AF661519

HEARTbreak Over DOKLAM

Major General Dipak Mukherjee

Vitasta
LET KNOWLEDGE SPREAD

Published by
Renu Kaul Verma
Vitasta Publishing Pvt Ltd
2/15, Ansari Road, Daryaganj
New Delhi - 110 002
info@vitastapublishing.com

ISBN 978-93-86473-28-8
© Major General Dipak Mukherjee, 2018
MRP 395

All Rights Reserved.
No part of this publication may be reproduced, stored in a retrieval system, or transmitted in any form, or by any means—electronic, mechanical, photocopying, recording or otherwise—without the prior permission of the publisher.
All persons portrayed in this book are fictitious. Any resemblance to real persons, living or dead, is purely co-incidental.

Editor Veena Batra
Cover and layout by Somesh Kumar Mishra
Printed by Vikas Computer and Printers

To my grandsons, Ayan and Yushaan.
May they keep the lights of life glowing
as they grow and live through this fascinating
and challenging century.

Contents

Acknowledgements

I am thankful to my family who insisted that I write more books.

I am grateful to Bill and Mary Chick of East Croydon, UK. Their enthusiasm and encouragement was indeed motivating.

I wish to thank my publisher Renu Kaul Verma who heads Vitasta Publishing in Delhi. She always encourages writers who fulfill the core value of Vitasta which is—Let Knowledge Spread.

Papri Sri Raman,who edited my last book spared no pains to ensure that this book too shapes up well. My heartfelt thanks to her.

Finally, with deep appreciation and gratitude,I thank Veena Batra who took great care while editing this book. With her vast experience and professional acumen, she has greatly contributed towards shaping this book with her value additions.

Singapore Management Academy An Incubator for Millennials

'My dear students,

'Today, as you step out of the campus of Singapore Management Academy which is akin to an incubator of knowledge sharing, you join the illustrious group of our alumni all over the globe.

'This farewell is an expression that we shall miss you. Your chirpings, blended with healthy mischief and banter, your energy resounding in the corridors of this institution, your laughter, your overnight stays while you performed plethora of business solutions… all will be missed. A fresh batch will fill your vacuum. The old order changeth, yielding place to new. The snowball of life will role on.

'So, go forth into the dynamic, challenging, at times unforgiving, fascinating world of business management, of creativity and wealth creation. Go forth and make the world better, fairer, inclusive, more charitable and therefore kinder. The hard power of wealth creation must blend with the soft power of good human values. May the road rise up to meet you; your wisdom and value systems lead you. May the tail winds of life take you forth.

'As you enter the real world of competitive professional life, changes...big changes in life will be inevitable. Do not only manage the changes but adopt, adapt and accept them, with grace, confidence and equanimity. You will now enter the start point of a new learning curve.

'This graduation batch has been groomed in this fine institution for the last two years—very carefully, imaginatively and skilfully. Thereafter, wherever you go, you shall be tackling projects after projects, presentations after presentations and their implementation. Never dither or fear. Remember how unsure you were when you walked into these premises. How many skills you have acquired, how hard you have all worked and how much exposure you all got here. You are all well trained, capable and empowered people now.

'You all worked together as teams comprising of nationalities of Asian, European and other continents. You all are a globalised work force. You are also in the fascinating century of the rise of Asia, rise of the third world, blending with the skills, technologies, and work ethos of the developed world. It is a century in which human beings are trying to rise together, such as never happened earlier with such intensity.

'The future dawn of human development will also now come from the eastern horizon, from where the sun shines first. You all are the millennials, the twenty-first century *youngistans*. Your horizons will be forever expanding.

'Be a great team member as you develop your leadership skills for a higher calling. You cannot be one without the other. Be motivated and also motivating. You cannot be one without the other. Be capable professionals as well as great dads, moms, husbands and wives. No fun of being one without the other. Earn well, but be charitable and kinder to lesser mortals. No point of being the first without the second. Let the world be your oyster, yet make it fairer. Whenever you leave an organisation, leave it in a better state.

'So far, for centuries, humanity has been suffering from

a disease known as *Earthritis*. The joints between civilisations and continents have been feeble and disjointed. The twenty-first century and globalisation processes are trying to cure this disease by seeking jointmanship. Singapore is in the joint for a future Asia. Your generation are the doctors who will cure the Asian *earthritis*.

'We have endeavoured to put the seed of knowledge and skills in you. The seed will now develop, assimilate the air, earth, and water and convert itself into a plant. The practical world will now make the plant grow and blossom. There will be storms, floods, draught as well. Such is the law of nature. As you grow, plant, groom and nurture more seeds and be a good leader.

'The environment today is packed with information, knowledge, data. You can Google and find out what Aristotle had for breakfast or how many children Alexander or Changez Khan sired (Laughter). That was on the lighter side. The line between knowledge and wisdom may look thin but is actually very significant. My entire faculty and I wish you great wisdom. Spread the light...light the lights around you as you move on in life.

'Everyone aspires to reach the pinnacle of their profession. There is nothing wrong with that. But the vacancies up there will always be very few. Can one also aspire for a successful, meaningful life? The definition of success needs to be defined by each one of us, for our own selves. There maybe so many other aspects of life as critical as success and happiness in our multifaceted lives.

'Think of the graduation just as a goal post which you are just crossing. It is the first phase of your moving into an environment where you have to live out the real life. For the first few years, try to learn more. To do so, you must listen more, reflect more and thus imbibe more. As you grow, succeed and prosper, make humility your centre of gravity. Never become proud, arrogant or unprincipled.

'So run through your professional life with perseverance.

Run this marathon gracefully, sportingly. Be proud of having run it well. Some may run this marathon better, learn from them. Many would do less. Never whip yourself to comparison. It doesn't matter. While in this marathon, lead a value based, happy personal life. Life is essentially about giving back a bit more than you have received. God bless you all.'

Just as he concluded, the screen on the stage prominently showed a slide

KNOWLEDGE IS PROUD THAT HE HAS LEARNED SO MUCH,
WISDOM IS HUMBLE THAT HE KNOWS NO MORE.'
—William Cowper

After the farewell address, Ayan, Arvind, Naveen, Sneha and Radhika met at the *Relax & Cool* bar of the Academy. The bar was crowded, cacophonic and full of scholar students. All were excited as well as nostalgic about the past two fruitful, sabbatical years at the Academy. They were all raring to go confidently into the profession of Business Management.

'Wasn't it an excellent address?' exclaimed Sneha. 'The Dean covered many aspects which he thought were relevant to us. Spoken like a true professor and a father figure. He tried to give us a panorama of the future environment in which we will be launching ourselves.'

Ayan reflected, 'Quite so. He blended the practical realities of the business world with the need to be good, creative human beings. He stressed on the need to contribute towards a better, more inclusive external world and be rooted to the realities all around us. He also subtly tried to caution us about the changes and challenges we shall have to tackle in the real world, which we shall soon be confronting.'

'Yes Indeed,' said Naveen, chipping in. 'I liked the way he reiterated that we all will be active participants in the ongoing process of the rise of Asia which would be a fascinating journey, full of prospects as well as challenges. He linked it as an essential component of the globalisation process. He explained that it can be done with the help of the skills, technologies, work ethics and efficiency of the developed world. Many a times, people try to view the rise of Asia narrowly as East versus West, as a challenge to the hegemony of the developed Western world. In fact, rise of Asia means rise of the world. One cannot be without the other—as the professor usually tells us.'

'All this is fine, goody, goody stuff,' quipped Arvind, with a sarcastic smile. 'The business world is a veritable jungle. It is not such a professorial world out there. In that jungle, it is survival of the fittest. To survive, as well as prosper, one has to be ruthlessly focused. Just reflect that the subject of Business Ethics was the easiest part of the syllabus, wasn't it? We could score easy marks by glibly glossing over morality, compassion for all stakeholders, environmental concerns, inclusiveness and all such sermons.

'*Yaar*, the world of wealth creation is akin to a Roman stadium when gladiators fight each other to the end. The mass of the spectators who are also stakeholders, sit around cheering only the victors and jeering at the losers with scorn. It is a win or lose situation, an unforgiving environment, with a grounded, cruel realism which is as cold as the backside of a duck in a pond.'

'Do not exaggerate so much Arvind!' exclaimed Sneha. 'You need to redefine and drastically modify your ideas of what a successful life implies. If the business management world is such a toxic jungle, then all the more we need to detoxify the profession as the professor suggested with such passion. Isn't that how we should interpret the farewell address?'

'No Sneha, I am not exaggerating *yaar*. This may be to an

extent, but not in essence. I am responding with a different perspective. Do not think of the global business environment as a distinct, productive, creative, stand alone endeavour. Come on, dwell deeper. When you see business in conjunction with political power play, as part of geo-economy, geo-strategy, you are dealing with an insidious, ruthless system. Add the ingredient of military industry, arms lobby amidst large parts of the chaotic world and you get a dangerous recipe. Finally, when environmental degradation comes in the way of seamless wealth creation, dangerous games are played. The destiny of future generations will get affected by present prosperity. Get real guys,' retorted an agitated Arvind.

'Come on Arvind,' pleaded Radhika. 'It is not such a bad world. It is neither an ideal world. It is a human, fault-lined world. Besides, the bulk of the creative, productive people are good human beings. They too give back quite a bit of what they earn. Isn't the world today better than what it was a century or more ago or than the medieval times?'

Before Arvind could prolong the discussion further, Ayan smiled and said, 'All of you missed having a look at Professor Miss Wang. She passed by twice, wearing such a smart skirt and a beautiful top. What a ravishing sight she was. 'And Arvind, for two years you have been subjecting us to your heavy stuff committing *bheja fry* on us. Relax *yaar.* Chill... We have completed the course. All of us have been placed in good jobs. Hey Radhika, Sneha, what would you like...coffee or green tea?'

'Oh Ayan, the ever chivalrous, cultured friend. Tea will be fine for both of us. It will be great if tea is accompanied by a few tuna sandwiches. And I am not paying,' said Radhika. Ayan come back with a tray of tea and sandwiches.

'Thanks Ayan,' said a beaming Sneha.

'So we guys will soon move out into the yonder world for our respective jobs,' said Naveen. 'However, both the ladies of our group have different plans. I must say that the placement wing of our Academy is a competent lot. What a neat job they did. The best global companies came to interview us. There has been ninety percentage placements at the campus itself, in the first effort.'

Ayan looked at Sneha. 'You are going back home to Dehradun and have preferred to chill out for a while. If you wanted, you could have got a good offer in Singapore itself.'

'Yes indeed. I shall work at home reorganising my dad's work. He is setting up a modern polyclinic in the Doon valley. It will have a state of art heart centre.'

Arvind looked at Radhika. 'Radhika has all the luxury of taking her time to decide. I am sure her rich doting dad will encourage her to start some entrepreneuring venture here in Singapore. Uncle is a big shot here and Radhika his only child. Lucky lady.'

Radhika smiled indulgently.

Arvind looked at Ayan and Naveen. 'You both are from army families and your dads would be retiring soon. Both of you have starting pay offers larger than the pay they received after three decades of military service. Isn't that an achievement? They both must be proud of you.'

Amusement lined the boyish face of Ayan.

'Many times Arvind, I have noticed that you tend to grasp the arse both ways. I hope by virtue of the august company of the four of us, you change your attitude now. If you don't do so, soon you will develop the habit of walking backwards,' joked Ayan.

Everyone laughed loudly with Arvind too joining in. The comradeship and frank bonhomie in this group of five was very intense and healthy, despite many differences of views. Two years of association had grown into a strong friendship. They could speak their minds to each other, without fear or hesitation, with honesty and transparency.

'Come on Ayan, we all are issued with an arse, so where is the difference?' retorted Arvind.

Ayan said laughingly, 'We all have one but you are one. But I must clarify this Arvind,' he continued, 'The honour, elan, dignity of life lived by our dads, and I speak for Naveen also, was unique. The element of leadership required while leading subordinates on missions involving sacrifice of lives and limbs for the nation, the spirit of adventure, daring, risk management, getting the best out of the human resources, continuous training, motivation and organisational commitment are unmatchable. Their pay was less but they lived honourably and brought up their children very well.

'In fact,' Ayan pressed on, 'the world of business management needs to learn so much from military management apart from concepts of democratic, secular nations. Everything from mission statement, environmental analysis, tactical and strategic studies, detailed plans, contingency plans, small team operations, resource management, human resource optimisation, logistics, IT, to morale, *espirit-de-corps*, leadership, communication skills, leading by personal example—what is not there to learn from them? Finally, they have patriotic commitment which enables them to give so much for so little in return. No profession can match the military.'

Sneha gently put her hand on Ayan's shoulders. It was a reassuring touch of a friend who understood.

'I agree my friend,' acknowledged Arvind. 'Well said indeed.' This time he appeared genuine.

Naveen showed a thumbs up sign towards Ayan. Radhika too was listening very intently. She lavished a beautiful, soothing smile on Ayan.

Having lived in Singapore for the last ten years with her parents, Radhika was a regular source of home food, at least once a month for her group. Radhika's mom was a great, fun filled lady with extraordinary cooking abilities. Often she cooked homemade snacks, neatly packed, enough for five hungry people. Her father was rich, with a big heart. He doted on his daughter and always ensured that there was enough money in her account. Radhika, always aware that her friends had comparatively limited resources, would take a larger share of the eating out expenses. Arvind too, being from a prosperous business family in Noida chipped in accordingly many times.

'So what is your future plan Radhika? You did not participate in the placement interviews,' asked Arvind.

'*Yaar*, I do not want to plan my future. Let it all happen. I will take a year's break and travel.'

'Okay, you have the luxury, so indulge. But you must have a vision of what you want to do with life.' Arvind pressed on.

'Actually, I am confused. Perhaps the most indecisive people are those who are born with a silver spoon in their mouth. Maybe I am a start-up person who does not know from where to start at the moment. Soon I may find out. I may also go in for a doctorate in management.'

'Which aspect of management would you like to research in,' asked Ayan with interest.

'Aah, maybe something to do with organisational behaviour and ethics in business management, so as to further refine the art and craft of Business Management in the twenty-first century.'

'Wow! great subject to work on,' acknowledged Ayan admiringly.

'It is too serious a subject. Life is waiting to offer you too many possibilities to be ignored, dear Radhika,' said Arvind.

'No one climbs Mount Everest for money, Arvind. Radhika wants to do something entirely unconventional but noble and challenging. Go ahead Radhika. Climb every hill, climb every mountain, till you find your dream,' encouraged Naveen.

'Thanks Naveen,' acknowledged Radhika with a sweet smile.

'Well Arvind, you maybe right or you may not be. Who can understand the mysteries of *zindagi ka safar*. Therefore, just travel and marvel at life, savouring it as well as suffering it. My *Ganesha* will see me through. Meanwhile Arvind, I prescribe *Hanuman Chalisa* for a typical Delhite like you,' quipped Radhika.

Ayan looked at Sneha. 'So you too want to get into research. Good for you. You love to study and get into the depths of the matter. You are too sincere and scholarly type to be seeking a job yet.'

'Yes *yaar*. The MBA course has made me realise that there is so much more to learn yet. I feel that the subject of skill development and employment generation of people in rural and semi urban India needs a lot more study and research. My desire is to take on this subject to research on. My dream is to do that in a good university in UK,' replied Sneha.

Ayan nodded smiling. 'In fact, my sister Dia did her doctorate from University of Cambridge on Astrophysics.'

'Wow! That is perhaps the toughest subject anyone can dare to take. She must be brilliant. I must contact her for inspiration and guidance,' replied Sneha with enthusiasm.

'Yes, I shall organise that. You will get along very well with her. She too is crazy about research,' said Ayan encouragingly.

'What will you do after that? Surely you would need to take up a good job,' queried Arvind.

'Well, I would love to teach after that in any institute of excellence,' replied Sneha with confidence and clarity of purpose.

'Great *yaar*,' encouraged Naveen. Ayan nodded with approval.

Suddenly Radhika got up and addressed the group as if she was the female version of Mark Anthony.

'Friends, aspiring about-to-be project managers, consultants, investment bankers and countrymen. I have lent you enough money for the last two years, not counting the food you all hogged from my mother's kitchen. If you all are honourable people and even Arvind is an honourable man, you will return my money, I mean my dad's money. I am not here to bury your debt but to recover it. Arvind is looking at me as if he will stab me. I don't want to die saying *Et Tu* Arvind, and hence, I hereby write off all your debts, because, I repeat, even Arvind is an honourable man.'

As Radhika finished her Romanesque, rather short speech and sat down, the entire lot at the bar got up and gave her a standing ovation. They all had a healthy respect for this group of five bright chatterboxes of the 2008 batch. The business school band played the song from the film *Sound of Music*.

'Edelweiss, Edelweiss, Every morning you greet me,
Small and white, sweet and bright,
You look happy to meet me....
Edelweiss Edelweiss, bless my homeland for ever.'

As the group of five, which they were popularly known as, got up, Radhika said softly, 'Thank you Ayan, Naveen and Arvind for treating Sneha and me as friends, comrades and not as objects, which usually is the case in real life. We do forgive you dears for a little bit of acceptable flirting done in jest. If you didn't do that then we would have been a little disappointed. Ha! Ha!' All five had moisture in their eyes.

Ayan's Career Switch

Ayan had just completed his check-in at Mumbai International Airport. He had over an hour to spare before boarding from Gate 18A.

The short journey from Domestic Airport took nearly an hour, including waiting for the transit bus. There were about thirty foreign tourists in the bus. Seeing an elderly, perhaps a French lady standing in the overcrowded bus, Ayan stood up and offered her his seat. She accepted the offer gratefully, though with some surprise. Perhaps she was not used to such normal niceties from most Indian males, in this land of Karma.

The circuitous drive was embarrassing indeed. Ayan watched people yawning, burping nonchalantly without covering their mouths. Some were speaking loudly even when the person spoken to was barely two feet away. A few guys kept their hand luggage on the seat next to them despite so many standing. One person requested one of them to remove the handbag to enable him to sit, which was reluctantly complied with. The ride of over a kilometre was most embarrassing. Asia's largest slum sprawled on the other side of the low boundary wall enclosing the runway. It reminded the foreigners that India was a dreadfully poor nation. Ayan noticed smug smiles on the faces of some foreigners as they looked at each other.

Ayan said to himself, 'Mirror mirror on the wall, when the fucks will India stand tall.'

The British Air staff was efficient and caring. The food looked good and was served well. Ayan wished he could say the same about the taste. Being from an army background, he fondly remembered the English food in the Officer's Mess. Lovely golden fried cutlets, roasted chicken, scotch eggs, boiled vegetables with white sauce and garlic bread. And finally the tasty pudding. The British officers must have developed their taste buds for the flavours of Indian herbs and spices after colonising the country. They must have modified their bland dishes accordingly.

The flight to Baltimore, USA, was a long one. He was to join his merchant navy ship there. Ayan relaxed in his seat, closed his eyes and pontificated about where life was taking him. Literally so. He was not in control. This made him feel uncomfortable. This could not be the norm for he could not drift through life. He had to take charge. This could not be his lifelong career.

After leaving Mount St Mary's School in Delhi Cantonment, he and his small group of friends decided to join the Merchant Navy as Engineers. The heady mix of good money, adventure and globetrotting appeared very luring. They joined a four year Marine Engineering degree course in Pune. After completing the course they were promptly offered jobs as junior engineers in various prominent shipping companies.

Every year, for up to eight months Ayan sailed all over the world. Initially they sailed on ships over twenty years old. Sailing on such old horses was exhausting. Maintaining, running and repairing such a ship was a challenge. Remaining cocooned within the narrow confines of the ship with a small team of engineers, over such long periods, out on the seamless blue seas was stifling. He felt claustrophobic. Growing up as a child in various army cantonments, he had enjoyed a nomadic childhood in open, organised spaces with lots of security. The worst was when such old ships had to dry dock in a foreign port for maintenance. Ayan felt that this could not be his lifelong profession, however much some others may like it.

When sailing on a relatively new ship, life was better. Perhaps this is a well thought out strategy of shipping companies. As junior engineers, for the first couple of years, they have no better options to go anywhere else. So put them through the grind in an old ship. It makes professional sense because nothing can train, groom, and toughen junior engineers better than an old ship. Later as one clears the various prescribed tests and as one inches towards second engineer rank, one gets options to join other shipping companies offering better ships to sail. So offer them better choices periodically.

Ayan passed the various exams and became a third engineer, knocking the doors to become a second engineer in about a year. He had decided that this would be his last sail.

He remembered the discussion with his dad the previous year. He realised that his dad would retire in a year from the army. After thirty-eight years of service in the army and rising to the rank of a Major General, all he would have was a pension and a flat in Noida. An army career is exciting, dignified, and adventurous. It is laced with continuous exercise in leadership, training subordinates for missions, which may involve death and injuries. The ultimate management and leadership skills are those which demand the prospects of sacrificing life and limbs to achieve tasks. So, if anybody wants to be wealthy, one should not seek this profession.

Ayan had observed how his dad would be alternating between two years of peace posting and over two years in remote, dangerous border areas—insurgency prone areas. So his schooling changed every two years. He remembered his parents begging around in the better private schools for admitting their children. While in the midst of all this, his counterparts from civilian background would enter a good private school from KG level to class XII. Hence, children of military personnel had no choice but to learn how to deal with the dynamics of changing external environments and the flexibility of thought and actions to adjust cheerfully. So, very hesitatingly, he told his dad that he wanted to change his profession.

'Okay, take your call,' encouraged his dad calmly. 'Your career and your wife should be selected with greatest care, son. They make life worth living. Tell me Ayan, which is the subject which you liked most and have scored best in your studies so far?'

'It was the management capsule. I always scored an A plus,' replied Ayan, expecting to see a worried look on the face of his greying dad. It did not happen.

'Then go for it. Let it be in a very good institute of global standard. I saw the Indian School of Business in Hyderabad. That is the level I want. I am aware that Singapore is a country where some excellent centres of learning exist. Even if you want to go to Europe, USA, do so. Do not worry or hold yourself back. I can sell the flat in Noida to raise the funds,' replied his dad without hesitation.

Ayan knew that apart from that flat, his dad had no other property, so if he sold it he would have no other option but to stay in a rented accommodation after retirement.

'No dad. We don't need to do that. I am saving reasonably from my sailings. By the time I leave the Merchant Navy, I would have saved enough to pay the hefty fees as well as for accommodation and food...or nearly so,' assured Ayan.

Ayan's dad looked at his son for some moments fondly. He had not quite liked the first career choice. He had waited patiently for Ayan to find his true potential. He, however, knew that his own experiences of challenges in the Merchant Navy would toughen Ayan physically and mentally. Now he knew that his son had found his compass.

Ayan took a year off. He studied very hard and prepared for his GMAT tests. He would only appear for the formal competitive test once he was fully satisfied. He had to clock over 700 marks to get admitted in a worthwhile Management School.

Based on his good score, he got a call letter from Singapore Management Academy (SMA) and later from the Indian School of Business, Hyderabad. The Singapore course was to start in Jan while the Hyderabad School was to start in May. He did not want to lose six months. So he promptly accepted the Singapore offer. He could manage to meet the expenses in Singapore better too, due to a possible grant of scholarship. His parents were very happy.

His Dad said, 'Ayan, Singapore is the geographical centre of gravity for the future rise of Asia in this century. It is the most organised, disciplined and efficient entity of Asia. It gives the highest priority to education and good governance. That is the place to go and grow.'

Ayan remembered his parents coming to see him off at Mumbai Airport for his journey to Singapore. Maa was her usual composed self, always positive about the future of her family. She always displayed an uncanny self control, self confidence even when dad used to depart on postings to conflict prone regions, remote insurgency infested areas. In her private space, she was regular with her prayers.

Dad was fidgeting around, emotional about his son's departure abroad. He pressed on with his conversation as if to utilise every moment before parting from his son.

'You know Ayan, Singapore realised India's potential before Indians themselves did. Under Lee Kuan Yew it was instrumental in getting India admission to the Association of South East Asian Nations (ASEAN). Singapore is the shining example of how strategic leadership and vision of one person has transformed it into a jewel of Asia. The British, while leaving Singapore had described it as a pestilential and immoral cesspool city. You will be surprised to know that Lee Kuan Yew had once sought India's help to build the Singapore military including its defence production capacities. India refused, not unsurprisingly, given the fact that it never possessed a strategic culture. Lee Kuan Yew considered India as a major player in Asia in 1950s, as well as the best passage to the Afro-Asian world. Singapore will always remain the model, reminding Asians of their true potential and motivate the region to rise in peace and harmony.'

'Dad,' replied Ayan, 'you sure have some knowledge on varied subjects apart from military matters.'

'In the military profession, dear Ayan, we conduct lots of studies. We study geography, economics, political affairs, governance, global fault lines, external as well as internal challenges, past and future conflicts etc. And yes, we study and practise most of the things taught in management study syllabi, with our own perspective. In our profession we never neglect humanity and social sciences. After all, military is an instrument of politics. Military conflict is all about achievement of politico-strategic aims. War is about people.

'Bye Ayan,' he said, giving him a tight hug. 'From tomorrow your life will change forever. The world will open up to you. Rise and shine. All the best.'

Aah, thought Ayan. Finally I am heading for an MBA course in Singapore. I had played this scenario over and over in my mind during the last three years while on board various ships.

He had booked an early morning flight from Mumbai to Singapore. After crossing a rather inquisitive officer at the Custom Department, he finally entered the main lounge area. Nearby was his boarding gate. It was here that he was to meet his friend Naveen. In a miraculous development, Naveen, from his marine engineering days had also got admission in the same batch of Singapore Management Academy. Ayan therefore had somebody he knew very well. That went a long way in making the butterflies in his stomach settle down.

Eventually Naveen turned up and both excitedly caught up with each other over a beer. In an hour, the boarding for the flight was announced. Ayan made a quick call to his parents before shutting off his mobile. Settling into the seat, he checked out the in-flight entertainment and looked for the Oscar awarded movies. He selected the film *Dead Poets Society*.

The Singapore Airlines flight gave Ayan the first flavour of his destination. Technically, he had been near Singapore many times before. The merchant navy ship would frequently anchor ten-fifteen miles away from the port, to refuel and load stores. Many a times, after a long day in the engine room, he would stare towards the Singapore coastline from the deck and promise himself that he would spend time in Singapore some day. So, finally it was happening. He happily bid adieu to Mumbai as the flight smoothly rose towards the early morning sky.

The professionalism of the flight staff was clinically perfect. He closed his eyes and reflected upon his four years of experience as a marine engineer. He had travelled around the world, seen all the continents and oceans. Now he had found his purpose in life. Suddenly Ayan felt a pleasant velvety touch on his right shoulder. The polite air hostess, with a smile that could launch a thousand ships, offered him choices for juices and some nuts and said, 'Enjoy and relax sir.'

'Oh thank you,' replied Ayan offering his best smile and dreamy eyes. He remembered a girl in school who had remarked that his smile was so disarming, soothing and childlike. Mischievously he hoped she would touch him again when she brought the breakfast tray later. An Indian politician was travelling in the executive class. Half a dozen of his subordinates were sitting around in the economy seats around Ayan. They looked arrogant and crude. In fact, they were a combination of arrogance and servility, switched off and on as if by a button. When a couple of them at a time, for no rhyme nor reason, would get up and go to the politician, their gait and manners would be of extreme servility. Somewhat like a dog with its tail down. Having checked that their demigod was comfortable, as they returned they would switch on to the arrogance mode. This was to display to the *aam aadmi* in J class that they were *khaas aadmi*. Together with the pot bellied politician, the entire group seemed to be men of straw. A couple of times the air hostesses requested them to remain within the confines of J class and closed the curtain. They appeared a bit irritated with the usual razzmatazz associated with the typical VIP culture of India. If this was an Air India flight, no air hostess would have dared to mess with this group. VIPs in India at times display a mind and stature as small as a proton, thought Ayan. If these guys are not replaced with a system of meritocracy, India will continue to remain a country where hanky meets panky to rule over the system.

Ayan and his generation of Indians were very emotional about their country. They yearned for changes in India either democratically or, as a last resort by some sort of a revolution. The present status quo would downsize India to a pygmy nation with a huge geographical space. Such politicians were the bane of India. So many elected politicians as well as the unelected ones at national and state levels outshone each other in misleading from the front, misgoverning as they moved on in power, missing no opportunity for corruption. The gross national character was always to remain in deficiency mode. They lived in a political Siberia, a harsh, unforgiving expanse where you learn commando tactics to survive and flourish. Everything was secret. Nothing was sacred. Their existence was a form of bondage with a chain made of gold. They were bonded to loot and exploitation.

Ayan woke up from a short nap to the pilot announcing that they would be touching Singapore soon. As the flight gradually pulled through the clouds, the Singapore coastline become increasingly visible. He could see hundreds of tiny specks on the ocean. These ironically represented the merchant ships that had once been his world. It made him reflect on how small his world was in his last profession. He was so glad to be amidst the larger scheme of things in this world.

The plane touched down. It was probably one of the smoothest landings Ayan could recall, subtly representing the efficiency Singapore is known for.

Soon they were at the immigration which was a breeze as they were out very soon. While Ayan was loitering around, the ever so efficient Naveen had already ordered a cab. To Ayan's surprise it was a Honda Sonata, a luxury car in India, owned by the very privileged class. He anticipated a very high fare and glared at Naveen. However, within a few minutes he realised that all cabs were a Honda.

The first thing that struck them both was the super clean surroundings and the extremely fast speed at which the cars were being driven. The cab driver was cheerful, friendly and extremely talkative. He had a very different accent. They really had to concentrate hard to catch what he was trying to say. Nevertheless it was fun listening to him. He seemed to complete every sentence with a singing note which sounded like *Laa*.

The rooms where they were to stay were tiny, yet comfortable. It was amazing how they had provided all modern facilities in such a small space. The rooms were reflective of the country. Singapore really proved the saying that 'Small is Beautiful'. The rest of the day was uneventful as they rested and decided to call it a night after a meal at a nearby MacDonalds.

Next morning, another friendly talkative driver drove them to the Singapore Management Academy.

The SMA was very different from what both of them had anticipated. They were expecting a huge open ground with one huge building that ran from end to end, as were visuals of American and European Colleges that they had seen on the net. Obviously such lavishness in terms of area was impossible in Singapore. The Academy was in the middle of the city. The city's hottest party spot called Clark Quay was located nearby. The Academy had six different streams of study or schools. Each school had one posh looking building for itself. Their school was the 'Business School'.

They met a rather cool, cheerful guy named Sted, who was from the Admin team. Sted first asked them to register their names on a system and then offered to take them around the campus, which they happily accepted. Sted explained that all six schools were actually interconnected with each other via underground facilities. In fact, the actual college campus was primarily underground. How cool?

He took them there and to their surprise the underground facility was full of students. Some were huddled on benches in the corners and were studying intently. Some students had set up stalls to ask everyone to sign up for random extracurricular activities. There were food courts of different varieties—coffee outlets, stationery shops, gift shops and what not. Ayan and Naveen also saw groups practising sword fighting, skating and badminton. The entire underground campus was beautifully lit, air-conditioned and Wi-Fi enabled.

After a quick walk, they came back to the Business School. As if anticipating their thoughts, Sted asked if they felt like a beer. They of course said yes, thirsty after the walk in the humid Singapore weather.

Sted led them to a bar, right inside the Business School. The Bar was called *Relax & Cool.* Here they could see quite a number of students quietly sipping beer and doing their assignments. Everyone was so polite, cultured. Any eye contact invited a smiling response. All these visuals were something impossible to experience amidst the din, bustle and cacophony of campuses in India. Everything was so orderly and businesslike. The bar also had a couple of pool tables. Sted mentioned that it had a student band which played live music after 8 pm. There were student discounts and offers available. One just had to flash the MBA ID Card. Ayan and Naveen were highly impressed with what the Academy had to offer students. It would be fun to excel in the midst of such an excellent environment and facilities.

Arvind's Transition

Arvind was impressed with Singapore. Great infrastructure, clinically perfect layout, stamp of efficient governance everywhere. Have these people been para-dropped into this city state from somewhere else? Isn't this country a model of what Asia can be if other nations can rise up to it ? Arvind thought.

He had been reluctant to move out of India initially. He was born with a silver spoon in his mouth. His father along with two brothers ran a vast and successful real estate business in Noida named Esteem Homes. They lived as a joint family on the entire top floor of an exclusive super luxury block of Esteem Homes in Sector 83 of Noida. The entire floor consisted of three interconnected flats. The rest of floor space comprised of three large offices, a central temple, an ultra modern conference room, a catering section and a bar. The first floor of this particular block was modified for security personnel and administrative staff. Arvind's grandparents belonged to Dalhousie, a beautiful hill station in Himachal Pradesh. They still owned a fruit orchard and a palatial bungalow there.

Arvind had studied in Lawrence School Sanawar and did his B-Tech from Bangalore. Thereafter his father said, 'Arvind, I have plans for you. India is on the cusp of a major makeover. The global economy is undergoing tectonic spread. The compass of future is pointing towards the direction from where the sun rises. A fascinating future awaits your generation. Crack the GMAT well and go to any good institute you like. You need to become global rather than remain just a Delhiite. Hone your skills and learn everything you can over the next few years to be able to participate in the global economic resurgence of the twenty-first century. Your capabilities, intentions and ambition should be suitably built up.'

'But dad…' Arvind said mildly, 'Isn't there enough for me to handle in our vast business here? Even after doing an MBA abroad.'

'You need to question your assumption that real estate will remain as successful in the distant future. You need to differentiate between family legacy and future uncertainties. Every paradigm has an upward motion which flattens after an expiry date, and if you continue to reinforce the status quo the graph falls downwards. You will then need to change the model. That is what strategic thinking is all about. You need to always change to a new vision and proceed into new realities, from goal posts to goal posts.'

'But dad, India is going to become an economic giant of the future, isn't it?' argued Arvind.

'Hm…' pontificated his dad. 'I wish I was so sure of that. What India is really cut out to be, I wonder. How much do we have it in us to compete globally, I do not know. We will go somewhere, messing up, blundering as we move on. India's economy is being globalised, while its politics remains fossilised. Its status quo culture is averse to risk taking. Even if we are on the globalised train, we maybe behind in a three tier air conditioned coach somewhere. We will miss the first AC and Second AC coaches. We are still among the pygmies of the world in terms of technology. Except being synonymous in space exploration we are anonymous everywhere else. India has not invested towards building institutions, without which it cannot rise enough. The entire region of South Asia is hollow on basics. After all, how strong can a structure be if the edifices are weak?'

Arvind nodded his head overwhelmed by his dad's expectations of his son. He was pensive and apprehensive. He was to leave the family ivory tower—its comforts, luxuries and securities; and gallop into the world and take it on. He did not visualise the future in the manner his dad did.

He did not want to go too far away from Delhi. He studied hard. A professional expert on GMAT was hired to coach him. He was fairly good in studies. He had done well in his school at Sanawar. He was a good debater, good in sports and pretty handsome. He now knew that he could no longer sit on his backside and look after his dad's business worth hundreds of crores, yet so soon. His GMAT scores enabled him many choices. With money being no issue, after browsing through various global institutions, he decided to go to Singapore as advised by his friends. 'Why go too far away to USA or Europe?' they said. 'Singapore is near enough and good enough and qualitatively the best in Asia.'

The Maserati car was taking Arvind from Noida to the Indira Gandhi International Airport, T3 Terminal. On the way, Arvind longingly looked at advertisement hoardings of Esteem Homes. One huge hoarding read 'Esteem Homes… An Eternal Experience', showing beautifully laid out multi-storeyed flats, row houses, parks, swimming pool, club house, nine hole golf course, tennis courts, cycling routes, a gym… the complete works. Another huge hoarding said 'Esteem Homes give you the esteem you never felt before.'

So I have to take all these to the next level, more diverse, more creative. Why was dad thinking so big for me? Hope I am up to all these expectations, sighed Arvind.

Sneha

Sneha was a sportsperson. She was good at squash and badminton. She had attended various National Cadet Corps (NCC) camps in school and attended the Republic Day Parade at Delhi. While she was graduating from Miranda House in Delhi, she did a mountaineering course from the Himalayan Mountaineering Institute at Uttarkashi, with distinction. Later she wanted to volunteer for a mountaineering expedition. Her parents dissuaded her.

She wanted to join the Army. She loved the idea of wearing a military uniform, loved the military elan and ethos. Inwardly she relished the notion of being able to stand shoulder to shoulder with male officers and outshine them professionally. She would enjoy having official command over men. The cheap notion of male superiority repelled her. But this idea too did not meet with much enthusiasm from her parents.

Her brother Govind had the same fascination for a military career. Strangely, he got motivated initially by watching a black and white Bollywood movie, on a Sunday afternoon on TV. He was a class XII student then. The film was *Hum Dono*. Later on, during the Kargil Operation, he saw it all at home, sitting amidst the comfort of the drawing room. Heroes like Capt Vikram Batra, Capt Manoj Kumar Pandey and so many other youngsters were seen doing the nation proud, in almost impossible situations. He saw the young generation of officers and men heroically trying to retrieve the blunders of its top military brass. made by their lack of strategic thinking and the inept resources provided to the armed forces. The clarion call of these young heroes, sons of the soil of India, touched his heart. Capt Vikram Batra died fighting the enemy. He had said, 'Either I will come back after hoisting the tricolour or I will come back wrapped in it, but I will be back for sure.' This really inspired Govind as well as Sneha.

Govind prepared very hard for the entrance examination to the Indian Military Academy, Dehradun. He got through. The subsequent grilling at the Selection Board Allahabad was intense and very elaborate indeed. He got selected. His dad grudgingly accepted, knowing that Govind could not be stopped.

Sneha was glad for Govind. However, deep within, she felt a bit bad. Maybe the next generation of girls would be difficult to hold back. She was now more determined in demanding her space to decide about her future. Her father was an eminent cardiologist and mother, a teacher. They were an ideal couple indeed, one complementing the other with dignity and respect for each other.

Sneha was determined to study abroad. Her childhood friend Radhika had studied with her up to class VII in Welham's Girls School in Dehradun. Later on, Radhika had left India for Singapore along with her parents. They settled down there. Sneha and Radhika remained in touch, sharing all their views and thoughts with each other. Radhika had later motivated Sneha to come to Singapore. Together they could do MBA perhaps. Sneha was so excited at this prospect that she spared no efforts to crack the GMAT test. Their parents were well acquainted with each other. With such friends being local guardians of Sneha, her parents had no hesitation in allowing their daughter to go abroad to Singapore.

Sneha told her mother, 'Now please stop this business of looking for a son-in-law. Please give me my space to decide about my life. Please equate me with Govind as far as my dreams are concerned. I shall always consult you and papa about all important issues. But please trust me with my decisions. You have done a great job in bringing up your two children. I will never let you down. Don't hold me back for mundane reasons Maa.'

Her mother stroked her hair affectionately. 'Go and pursue your life Sneha. Please accept the fact that as parents we could not bring ourselves to let you join the army. Later, one day, you will appreciate this better.'

'May I come in Papa,' asked Sneha, gently knocking on the door of her father's study.

'Come in my sweetheart. Oh you look cute. But you also look serious and a bit worried. Sit down. I too need a break from studying the complexities of a few of my patients. Heart is such a complex act of creation in a human body. So much more of research needs to be done!'

'How did you fathom that I am worried Papa?'

'It is simple. We are genetically interwoven. As a kid, whenever you were worried or disturbed, you used to come to me and sit on my lap quietly for a while. A good tickle from me, followed by your shrieking laughter and you used to be fine.'

'Papa, I will be leaving home for Singapore next month. Govind also has left home. Hope you and maa will not miss us too much?'

'Sneha, my dear, life is cyclic and we are all cyclists,' said Papa affectionately patting her shoulders.

'You know, once when we were in Panchmarhi, I saw two birds searching for a place to nest and bring up the soon–to-be born babies. They found that the safest place to nest was amidst the creeper plant on the walls of our porch, opening towards the garden. They feverishly worked to build the nest, gently rebuking me if I got close. In a few days time, they laid two small, brownish, spotted eggs. While the mother bird remained busy warming the eggs and protecting them, father bird looked after the sustenance. We mentally adopted the two eggs as our son and daughter. We were recently married. Very soon the kids came out. The parent birds become tense about their security, food and later teaching them how to fly.

'Eventually, the two birds flew off. The empty nest remained like an abandoned, dilapidated home. We never saw the parent birds again or maybe they could have been the same ones who came again next year. We too are simple, loving, protective parents. Perhaps that is why we could not allow you to join the army. You go and find your dreams. Our job now is to remain steadfast behind you, support you and most importantly pray for you. Give me a hug *yaar*,' concluded her papa.

Sneha had tears in her eyes. 'Don't worry Papa,' she said hugging him tight. 'You and maa have ensured that Govind and I can look after ourselves and each other. I will be fine. I am a bit unconventional in my thinking but deeply rooted to the values I have got from you both. Just think of me as another son not as a daughter.'

'Love you Sneha.'

'Love you too and love you two,' laughed Sneha clarifying the pun.

Govind was really glad for his sister. He was posted to a Medium Artillery Regiment in a remote, high altitude region of Arunachal Pradesh.

'Hi Govind. How are you doing up there, where even the *Eagles Don't Dare* and where no humans reside?' queried Sneha, loudly and affectionately.

'Oh, we are fine here. It is such a fulfilling experience to be here. Wherever the *Eagles Don't Dare*, the Indian army dares. Sneha, you need to speak more loudly for me to hear you well. I am yelling.'

'Me too Govind. How do you spend your time?'

'Lots to do, despite the rarefied, oxygen deficient air up here. We have to keep a large area under observation and well covered by the only artillery guns which can do well here which are the Bofors. We patrol around, maintain our equipment, constantly train ourselves, have flag meetings with the guys on the other side. They are on a plateau region while we are atop our side of steep Himalayas, giving them a great geographical advantage.

'How are they generally, Govind?'

'Well, I don't know for sure what they think of India per se but they do display a grudging professional respect and acknowledge our sense of commitment despite some serious disadvantages we operate under. They know that our response will always be pretty effective. They have their job to do, we have ours. Things overall seem to be okay for the time being.'

'Take care brother,' exclaimed Sneha.

'It is great, really thrilling up here. This is actually professionalism. Okay Sneha, bye. My quota of time for talking is over. All the best in Singapore. I am so happy for you.'

'Bye Govind, take care.'

Sneha felt proud of her brother. How keen I was to join the army. That band of wonderful young people of India, so much *josh* and spirit to take on challenging assignments under heavy odds, difficult terrain and weather. Their exemplary penchant to give so much for so little in return, their romanticised love for the nation, she pondered.

Sneha wondered that if the junior managers, middle level executives, managing directors, senior executives could be sent for a week long organised training sessions with military institutions or formations, how much it would benefit them.

ଓଃଥ

She settled down in Singapore. When Radhika received her at the swanky airport, it was a great relief. She spent a couple of days at her house. Radhika's parents were very happy to meet her again. Sneha felt at home in Singapore.

She got accommodation in a locality nearby. Radhika had selected a flat that Sneha was to share with two other girls. One was a cute Malaysian girl named Su and the other was a Bengali girl from Kolkata, Mishti. Mishti means sweet, which she actually was. Both of them were working in Singapore. Su as a librarian, while Mishti was a dentist in a polyclinic nearby.

Frequently, over the weekend, Radhika would take Sneha home. Radhika's mom was a great cook. They were a close family. Radhika would treat her parents as friends—fighting, arguing, making up, laughing and frolicking.

Realising that Sneha was very intense about her studies, Su and Mishti were always concerned about not disturbing her. Sneha felt comfortable with them. On return from their work late evenings, they would smile encouragingly at Sneha, deep in her studies. They would put the TV on low volume. One of them by turn would brew coffee and keep a steaming mug near Sneha. Often Sneha would put on some soothing Rabindra

Sangeet songs as she studied. Mishti and Sneha would prepare a typically Indian dinner of egg curry with rice or *chappatis*, *dal*, chicken curry and fish fry whenever they could buy good fish. Su usually would have had dinner at the local eating place near the library. At times, she would bring dinner. On such occasions they would eat together, sharing each other's meals.

The MBA course was very intensive, multipronged and open ended. Subjects were taught by a variety of methods. There were visiting professors and guest speakers who were extremely knowledgeable, while some were awesome. The teaching faculty were extremely competent, friendly and cheerful. They were always well dressed, meticulous in their gait and deportment. The horizon of learning was vast, one opening up to others in a never ending learning curve. The infrastructure and facilities at the university were world class. There was something special about the atmosphere of Singapore.

ଓଃ

After completing the MBA Course, Sneha got a response to her application for research and study in Cambridge University, UK. The Nehru Foundation shortlists candidates and after a very exhaustive selection process, sponsors one candidate each on various subjects for research and higher studies in the University. To be able to do so is the ultimate dream of academic oriented young boys and girls in India.

She was initially so happy to have been included in the first short list. Then nervousness engulfed her. Only one candidate would be selected in her subject from India. How could she be the one? No chance. The thrill and excitement of her parents made things worse. They appeared pretty sure that she would be selected, particularly her maa. They contacted an astrologer from Jammu. He was positive that Sneha was destined for studies abroad as Saraswati, the Goddess of learning was in a favourable planetary position.

'That's all nonsense Maa. Things don't work that way. I see no reason why I should be the one to be selected. Many others too are so good in India. You are not aware of how brilliant so many others are. Surely Saraswati, the Goddess of learning, would only encourage meritocracy and not indulge in favouritism. Makes no sense to me.'

Dad interjected. 'That is true, my dear. But how can you assume that in your subject you are not the best. Your subject is your passion. Your love for it is unconditional. You have forsaken such good pay packages after your MBA and displayed your deep penchant for further studies. That is what they will observe during your interviews. In this profession of wealth creation, you wish to research in greater depth the critical issues relating to India's growth. Rise of Asia is critical for a better world. Rise of China and India are critical to achieve this. Your subject hits the nail on this essential paradigm shift. Therefore, your urge for meaningful research on the subject of skill development, employment generation of rural and semi-urban Indians, may be quite appreciated. So you stand a good chance. Buck up.'

'But Baba, I don't think I am so great in conversation. Others are so articulate and stylish,' moaned Sneha.

'You are wrong there sweetheart. You are not great when conversations are light, casual and shallow. But trust me, on grave, thought provoking, challenging issues, you stand out as a class apart.'

'Hah, that is a typical dad speaking. Your opinions in the case are very subjective.'

'Believe me Sneha, while mostly this is so, on this particular issue I am spot on. You should be on your way to Cambridge if you believe what I am saying now.'

Maa butted in. 'Sneha, some goals are so worthy that it is glorious to have a crack at them, even if one does not succeed. You go into this interview process with your head held high, without worrying about the result. You have decided to do a doctorate. You would do that anyway. Think like that. Later on in life, you will reflect upon events which you never expected but they happened. This could well be one of them.'

'Wow Ma'am. So positive! A typical wishful Maa,' exclaimed Sneha laughing nervously.

'By the way Maa,' added Sneha, 'there will be scores of such mothers praying for their children during the final interview. Poor God! What will he do?'

'Okay, my forever leg-pulling daughter. When you answer multiple questions thrown at you during the interview, you imagine that God is asking those questions and you give honest replies, emanating from your soul. Thereafter, let God decide. Okay? Now shut up and prepare yourself for the interview.'

Sneha's Interview for Cambridge University

Sneha reached the sprawling palatial building with a huge compound located on Akbar Road in New Delhi. The venue for the interview for the Nehru Foundation Scholarship Scheme was so colonial, so grand that Sneha felt intimidated. She wondered why on earth she had got into this messy situation. The dream of studying in Cambridge University was just an unrealistic fantasy, a pipe dream. What would be the questions they would ask; how would she be able to tackle them? She had shared her concerns with Radhika. Radhika behaved just like Maa and made things worse.

'Sneha, just be your natural self. Remain *bindass*. You grossly underestimate yourself. You do not realise your potential. Had I been a boy, I would have booked you for marriage *yaar*, believe me. When you understand the questions clearly, answer from your mind. When you do not grasp some questions fully and you are not too sure, answer from the depths of your heart, fearlessly. Do not show any fear of not being selected. Somehow you have to stand out from the rest. You will, because you stand apart anyway.'

Sneha noticed that only ten candidates were called for that day. The process was to start at 10 am, and continue till 4 pm, with forty-five minutes of lunch break. She calculated that each candidate could be grilled for thirty minutes, at least. The interviews could also be extended to 5 pm.

She looked around the huge waiting room, which must have been a ballroom during colonial times occupied by some Governor General or a Lord. Four other girls and five boys were also there. They nodded to each other politely, wishing each other all the best. The girls were at least as nervous as Sneha. Surprisingly, the boys were not looking nervous. They perhaps, had better ability to hide their nervousness genetically or they were faking confidence, thought Sneha. Maybe the girls would lose out to these guys. How do the boys remain more cool, she wondered.

When Sneha was called in, two boys and a girl had been interviewed. Her watch showed 12 noon. She gulped down some water, took a deep breath and walked in.

Three smart, stately looking middle-aged ladies and three suave gentlemen in their sixties were seated around a semi circular, antique table. In front of each of them on the table were neatly placed water bottles, glasses, a clip board with a formatted sheet and some blank sheets and holders with various coloured ball pens. They smiled benignly as Sneha walked in. As she sat on the offered seat, she looked at all of them from left to right and thanked them.

'Sneha,' addressed the apparently eldest gentleman who sat in the middle. 'We shall be chatting with you for a while to understand you better. You have to help us to do so. We shall be asking you some questions, sequentially from left to right initially. Thereafter, if required, any of us can ask you further questions. Please relax. You have been shortlisted so we know you enough. Congratulations for being selected out of hundreds of aspirants.'

Sneha smiled and nodded.

Q 'How much knowledge do you possess at this point in time about your subject?'

Ans 'This subject has been close to my heart for a while. I have thought about it but my knowledge is very limited, Sir.'

Q 'In that case, why did you select this topic for your research?'

Ans 'Sir, it is for this very reason. It will help me start from scratch—start from grassroots levels. While doing my MBA, the subject of demographic dividend fascinated me when I heard the lecture on this subject from Dr Amartya Sen. I realised that this subject is as vast as are the regions of the world afflicted by abject poverty.'

The first speaker looked at the second gentleman and nodded. The second speaker took on.

Q 'Apart from the related subject of demographic dividend, what else motivated you to explore this subject in great depth?'

Ans 'Sir, may I take a little more time to answer this question?'

'Yes, please do so Sneha, we are all ears.'

'Thank you. The great challenge of the Mediterranean Divide, Sir.'

All six speakers looked up at Sneha inquisitively. Sneha now took off.

'Let us consider the Mediterranean Ocean as a symbolic divide between the Haves and Have Nots of the global population. Thousands of poor people with no education, no formal skills have been historically attempting to illegally cross the Mediterranean Divide, just to live, survive, to exist. They flee from their homes because of abject poverty, conflicts, strife and persecution. In their homelands there is no governance or corrupt governance, no skill training. Thousands perish in the Mediterranean while attempting to cross over. In India, there is the rural-urban divide of similar tragic proportions.

'Sir, under the globalisation process, goods and services are moving freely all over for better pastures and profits. Skilled manpower is similarly moving freely based on demand and supply. A huge part of global demography is left out of this journey of globalisation because they have developed no skills, while potentially being skilful. If the poor people in rural and semi-urban regions of the third world, including India are given training in skills they can learn and absorb, they can board the globalisation train and better their lives.'

'But that is a stupendous task in nations where governance is in deficit, to put it very politely,' observed another speaker. Now Sneha had caused a disruption in the process of the first six questions being asked sequentially. She had not done so deliberately though.

'That is why so much research is required in this subject of global concern. What can be a better place to do so than in the august, academic environment of Cambridge University, Sir? The issue is clear. Either we make a national and global effort to arm such people with skills and capabilities productively, or else others will arm them with weapons, explosives and destructive ideologies. Time is running against humanity. I am sorry to be sounding so pessimistic, but at this point in time I feel it this way. Maybe, after learning more about this from experts of international repute, I will feel more positive.'

Now the speaker in the middle of the semi circular table spoke.

Q 'I think we are at an interesting stage of this interview, or let us now call this a discussion. What are your views on the plethora of NGOs, from abroad and within India who are working on this experiment of skill development in India?'

Ans 'Coming to India, the abject poverty in rural India is as painful to watch as seeing many of them in semi-urban towns and metro cities. In urban and semi-urban India, non-skilled people provide domestic services to survive. NGOs are providing some short term balms. They are not expected to solve such massive problems. They can only mitigate them a bit.

The relationship between NGOs and government departments is tenuous and fragile. There are constant tugs-of-war over disbursements and funds so at times they get into collision mode. The challenge of demography is too vast to pass it on to the NGOs. What the government is doing is not delegation of responsibility; it is tending to negate its own responsibility. Ultimately, the government has to be the prime mover in empowering the impoverished masses through skill training. This is one challenging sphere of economic activity requiring maximum innovation, start-up, improvisation, research and unlimited imagination. It is about good governance. It is about building and utilising capacities and not about doles and freebies.'

There was a pause as the eminent team of interviewers looked at Sneha and then at each other. A stern looking lady who had been more on listening mode till then asked,

Q 'Don't you think that providing skills to such vast majority of people, over such vast spaces is very challenging under the present quality of governance?'

Ans 'It is. I wonder though whether it is out of our reach or have

> we not stretched ourselves enough? We have rendered vast numbers of Industrial Training Institutes (ITIs), redundant by neglect and insincere approach on this sensitive issue. Many government polytechnics are in a similar rotten state. They all can be resuscitated, reequipped and restarted with renewed focus. District Collectors and MLAs, MPs can be held accountable. In today's world when we feel the need what prevents us from tapping the developed world to help us, When they can be expected to help us with their high technology and management skills to produce defence equipment and state of art products, why not for skill development on low and medium level skills? Corporate Social Responsibility is finally coming of age in India. They can contribute enormously towards this as well as benefit from this enterprise. Global corporate giants will help us. So much can be done, since we have not even started doing this meaningfully.'

The last lady on the right looked intently at Sneha and smilingly joined in.

'Ok. Now let us leave the research angle and have an informal chat. Tell me young lady, why do people react differently to the same event?'

Sneha reflected upon the question for a few seconds.

'This is perhaps because all of us have a personal history, different personal experiences embedded in our persona. So we all have our own perspectives and assumptions, and when any event or issue confronts us, we need to challenge our assumptions and perspectives for their relevance to the context. Then we all can respond better or appreciate the perspectives and assumptions of others. Immediate responses will always lack that much of depth. Listening to others carefully becomes important.'

The eldest gentleman sitting in the middle looked at Sneha with great earnestness. The eye contact remained for a few seconds. Sneha quite liked this person.

'What is your weakest characteristic that concerns you?'

'I am not worldly-wise enough. While I can spot the good qualities in others, I am weak at identifying their faults.'

'What is your strongest characteristic?'

'I don't know as yet.'

'Which was the toughest question you encountered so far during this interview?'

'The last one.'

'Now this question may sound strange for this interview. One day, two thousand years later, how would the people think us who lived in the twenty-first century?'

There was a distinct pause for reflection by Sneha.

'They, after research on our existence, would wonder, "These idiots destroyed each other, believing in their respective books, written thousands of years before they were born. Some of the contents of those books were carried forward by word of mouth before the blighters learned to read and write"!'

The entire group smiled.

'There is a possibility of life in some other planets. One day, if they come and colonise human beings how will they treat us?'

'Maybe they will treat us as ruthlessly as human beings treated the pagans, the indigenous people of continents, aborigines, the fellow humans they captured and colonised.'

The group of interviewers remained pensive.

'Now to the final question. Why do you think we should select you for your research in Cambridge University with a scholarship?'

'I am not in a position to say why I should be selected over others.'

'A supplementary question, how do you assess your performance during this interview?'

'I wish I could do better than I did. I am not satisfied with my performance.'

Radhika–From Dehradun to Singapore

Radhika fondly remembered her early school years in the Doon valley. Their huge family bungalow was in Haathi Barkala area of Dehradun. It was a big estate with forty leechi trees. Two gardeners used to tend to the leechi orchard. The leechis were delicious, juicy. The two trees hugging the bungalow were reserved for family consumption, while three others were for sharing with some neighbours and relatives. The fruits from the rest of the trees were clearly demarcated, and used to be sold to a contractor, who promptly dispatched them for sale in prime localities of New Delhi. Her parents also owned a bungalow on a beautiful hill top in Mussourie in a dream like place called Clouds End.

Doon Valley is 120 km long. It has the Himalayas to its North and Shivalik Range to its south, Ganges to its East and Yamuna to its West. It is mentioned as part of a region called Kedar Khand, the abode of Shiva in ancient texts. It is said to have been the military academy where Pandavas and Kauravas had military training under Acharya Dron. In any case, it has the Indian Military Academy, RIMC, Doon School, Forest Research Institute and even today is the best educational hub of India.

It was so idyllic that Radhika as a child had felt as if in her previous birth too she was born in Dehradun. During summers, her family and some relatives moved to Clouds End bungalow near Mussourie. They would spend a couple of weeks there. She fondly remembered how all the children would carry packed lunches and hike around the areas nearby or trek up to Mussourie Mall road. Once, the entire family trekked up to Kalsi. She also fondly remembered a trek from Mussourie to Chakrata. The short but enjoyable climb from Rajpur to Mussourie via Oak Groves School was a frequent event. Years later, when she visited the Doon Valley she could hardly recognise it. Now as capital of Uttarakhand state it was so congested. Dehradun was like a once beautiful lady, now old, tired, gasping for life. Radhika no longer felt that she was born here in a previous life.

She completed her schooling in Singapore. Five years in this school transformed her into an efficient, organised and ambitious young girl. Her parents had established themselves very well soon after they shifted from India. Her father was an expert financial manager with a doctorate in global investment. Her mother was a trained, experienced teacher who established herself well in Singapore in a few years. The family was very progressive in their thinking and perspectives, while at the same time deeply rooted to Indian traditions and value systems. Her mother sang melodious *bhajans* as well as semi classical Bollywood film songs. Many evenings, she would play her sitar and practise her singing. The family loved to party and were excellent hosts. They presented the best face of India in the community around. All three of them had strong personalities and gave adequate space to each other.

With lots of property in Dehradun, Mussourie, Haridwar

and Rishikesh, and family businesses, her dad was rich, prosperous and well respected. He regularly donated towards the welfare of slum dwellers in India. The creation of a new state of Uttarakhand with the capital at Dehradun in 1998 was a huge financial boost for the family.

Radhika liked studying. While shopping in supermarkets of Singapore during weekends, her parents would leave her in the book shop for hours without any worry. They would always return to find her deeply engrossed in books. She would always pick up a few books for purchase. She would carry a notebook in which she would make extensive notes as she scanned books and magazines.

'What are the notings you make Radhika?' her mother would ask initially.

'Anything that tickles my mind, maa. They are random notes. What I will do with them, I don't have any idea,' she would smile and say.

Radhika graduated as a software engineer from an eminent institute in Singapore. She just could not decide about her career. One evening at home, she asked her parents to discuss what her career should be.

'Baba, I am at sea about what to do with my life,' she said, initiating the discussion.

'Why so?' queried baba.

'That is because she is spoilt for choices—the problem of plenty,' complained her mother. 'God knows how, where and when we will find a suitable boy for her. The clinically efficient environment of Singapore has made her very individualistic. We will have problems settling her in life.'

'It's not so bad Mum, as long you don't limit your search compass to Doon Valley or Delhi and Chandigarh and not be in a hurry. In any case, the environment in Delhi and Chandigarh is so pretentious, so artificial, so shallow. Everything is plastic.

It is annoying, baba. I want to discuss my career options and Mum starts on such a tangent where I have no interest now.'

'But both are interlinked, isn't it? Obviously career would come first. You can do anything as far as we are concerned. You still have to learn to deal with flexible circumstances of adjustments, giveaways as well as takeaways. Your upbringing has been so structured, so orderly, so civilised. The world outside this tiny great country is so bewildering. Look at the chaos that is India and its immediate neighbourhood. Look at you. You have all the idiosyncrasies of a creative person. You need to mix up more with people, the bulk of whom will be lesser mortals than you. It is in such an environment you have to choose an emotional anchor. You may not get a solitaire for a husband and may have to do with an American Diamond.'

'Baba, Mum is like the guy who knew how to write only one essay. That was about a football match. Even if the question is on a train journey, she will stop the train en-route near a village where children are playing football and write the whole essay on the football match. She just cannot help linking everything with my marriage. And by the way I will only settle for a solitaire. Not comprise with an American Diamond!' Baba laughed aloud, while Radhika giggled.

'One day, much later in life, when I am dead and gone, you as a mother will realise my predicament. Then, don't do the drama of looking at my photograph on the wall and tearfully say, 'Sorry Mum'.'

Baba exclaimed, 'Don't you know, she was seeing an old Bollywood film last night, Radhika? It is the effect of that.'

'Shut up and stop ganging up against me,' replied Mum with mock anger.

Radhika reached Singapore Management Academy at 9 am, fifteen minutes before scheduled time of reporting. She walked towards the Central Hall. Outside the Hall, tea, coffee were laid out for the new batch of 2008. Most of the students were already there introducing themselves to each other. From 9:30 am to 10:30 am the ceremony of self introduction would be conducted. At 11 am the opening address by the Dean would commence. Thereafter, the time was slotted till 1:30 pm for familiarisation with the layout of the premises, followed by lunch with the staff. From 2:30 pm onwards the process of documentation and collection of study material would commence.

Radhika observed the new entrants, her batchmates. It was quite a global composition. There were Indians, Singaporeans, Malaysians, Indonesians, mainland Chinese, Europeans, Americans, Sri Lankans, a few Koreans and two Japanese students. As they all met, no one could register the names except their citizenship. There would be enough time over the next week to know each other better. However, she was glad to note that there were two boys from India. The behaviour of one reeked of self confidence. The other boy looked decent, a bit nervous. In fact, he was quite cute in his manner, smile and disposition. Radhika noted that he was wearing black trousers and a smart blue shirt, both evidently new. Then there was Sneha. Smart, attractive, typically Indian. She was composed and intelligent looking. She carried herself with dignity and poise. 'Let us get through the formal introduction phase and then we could meet during lunch time,' she thought. She waved at Sneha who hurried towards her. They hugged.

Radhika held Sneha's hand and walked towards the two Indian students she had observed.

'Hi, I am Radhika. I am from Singapore. This is Sneha from Delhi.'

'Hello Radhika, hello Sneha, I am Ayan.'

'Hello ladies, I am Arvind from Delhi. Glad to meet you both. Quite an interesting batch it seems. It's nice to feel that we shall get to study and work with such a diverse bunch. Wow, it will be quite an experience.'

Sneha looked at Ayan. 'Which part of India are you from. Bengali, I suppose?'

'Well, this question is always difficult for me to answer. My dad has been an army officer, now retired. We never belonged to one place for more than two years ever. So I am a bit of a nomad who has lived and studied all over India. Presently living near Indore, where my parents are settled. I am like a salad bowl—a bit of Punjabi, Sardar, Bengali of course, North Easterner, tribal, Pahari, South Indian, Rajasthani etc.'

'A transparent, wholesome Indian,' chipped in Radhika, as they all laughed.

'We four could be a good group,' thought Radhika.

Just then another smart guy with a visibly short hair cut joined them. Ayan introduced him.

'This is my friend, Naveen. He is also from an army background. He is from Belgaum.'

'That should make us a group of five now,' observed Radhika, feeling comfortable.

The lunch hosted by Singapore Management Academy was very well organised indeed. The entire faculty and staff joined in. They went around in small groups and met every student of the new batch. Their behaviour was not at all formal. They appeared to be a bunch of casual beings, very friendly and warm. Yet, their dress, their gait and manner of conversation indicated their communication skills and an aura of professionalism. They were a very confident, dignified lot. Everyone was visibly impressed. Sneha felt very cool and comfortable. It was indeed a very wise decision to come to Singapore.

Arvind now realised the correctness of his dad's decision to move him out of his cocooned comfort zone and limiting environment of Delhi. He felt he was now being ushered into a larger horizon and seamless space of self development and broadening of vision. Two years of living here, studying with fellow students from all over the world, would make him a true blooded global citizen.

Thanks Dad, he acknowledged gratefully.

Ayan's Initiation into Globalised Workforce

Ayan was driving his car from Noida Sector 4 to Dadri. He was on a holiday in India after completing his MBA course in Singapore. The music system was playing a soft old romantic song of Hemant Kumar. He had lived in Delhi for quite a few years. It was only after he lived in Singapore for two years that he started feeling the chaos of Delhi. No helmets, no lane discipline, unimaginable insensitivity towards fellow human beings driving on the roads. There was no culture of highway driving. Whenever there were segments of the road which had no dividers there was utter pandemonium. It was like the lawlessness of the jungle. For getting a little advantage of a few yards over fellow drivers, all was fair. No culture, no civilised behaviour. It was all so crude and mean. Equally uncouth were those in the most expensive foreign cars. Enforcement agencies for traffic management were nowhere in control. It was a no holds barred chaos on a daily basis. One could be a helpless victim of road rage any time. No wonder every vehicle had a small Ganesha or Hanuman stuck in front of the driver's seat, or religious or cult slogans written behind the vehicle like *Maa ki dua, Sai Ram, Jai Baba Bhole Nath* etc. All citizens were invoking the divine to protect them from each other. Amazing indeed! Amidst such chaos, Hemant Kumar's love song of yesteryears felt almost spiritual and soothing.

At a particular point of this journey, a few kilometres from Dadri, there was a bit of commotion. Ayan noticed four knife-wielding goons trying to pull out a young girl from a three wheeler. The girl was resisting wildly, holding on to the vehicle. There was a partial traffic jam. What he did next was by instinct. He got out and tried to stop a few more vehicles, to no avail. He saw a Sikh truck driver trying to find a way out through a narrow space. He ran towards the driver and appealed, 'I am a Fauji, Sardarji, let us save this girl. Block the road with your truck and keep honking your horn, full blast.' Sardarji readily agreed.

Since there was no divider, the traffic was now jammed both ways. He ran around many impatient drivers and requested them all saying, 'We can save a girl from abduction, rape and murder. Just keep honking your horns.' People started responding as they felt this was the safest method to prevent the crime.

Meanwhile, the goons having been boxed in, kicked the poor girl, and were dragging her towards their car. They got really distracted by all vehicles blowing their horns. Ayan looked pleadingly towards the Sardarji to jump down from his truck and join him. He knew that a Sikh would not back off from such a situation. He had lived his childhood in military cantonments and knew the qualities of Sikhs.

The four goons realised that they could not drive their big car away due to the traffic jam. They saw the general mass of vehicles all around. Then they saw Ayan and a massive Sardarji with an iron rod approaching them. They left the bleeding girl as well as their vehicle and ran away. Ayan shouted asking others to nab the three. Everyone had cooperated in creating the jam and blowing their horns continuously, but they had no stomach to confront knife-wielding goons, anticipating that they may have pistols too.

Ayan and the Sardarji tried to give the goons a chase but they melted away. They both helped the girl and offered to take her to a medical centre for first aid. The girl pleaded to be just taken away from there and dropped in a locality a few kilometres away. Ayan suggested, 'Okay I will drop you wherever you want but first let us go to the nearest police station.'

The girl looked terrified at the suggestion. She said, 'Just please drop me home. God sent you two to help me this time. This itself is enough. God bless you both.'

Gradually, the traffic started sorting itself out and miraculously starting moving. The first lot of vehicles on both sides had seen what happened and were happy to have contributed towards the rescue job. As they passed Ayan and the Sikh, they paid them compliments with a polite salute. The Sikh responded enthusiastically with *Sat Sri Akal.* He shook Ayan's hands profusely and said, '*Shabash* Fauji Sahib. *Wahe Guru* would be pleased today. You made my day.' Ayan too thanked Kashmira Singh for his help. He then clarified to Kashmira Singh that he was the son of a Fauji actually.

'*Ikko hi gall hai* Sahibji,' replied Kashmira Singh.

The subsequent vehicles that passed by were unaware of what had taken place. As they slowly passed by, the drivers gave dirty looks to Ayan and Kashmira Singh. Kashmira exclaimed, 'Sahibji, *chalo chaliye; yeh log Punjabi mein hamein gali denge yeh samajh ke ki hamne yeh traffic jam kiya hai.*' He gave a warm hug to Ayan and jumped into his truck.

Suddenly Ayan realised that amidst all that had happened, one thing was singularly absent. No sign of any government agencies during the thirty minutes or so of a chaotic incident. He was also deeply disturbed by the fact that a citizen, a young girl, despite being a victim of an abduction and rape attempt, was mortally afraid to go to a police station. More often than not, many such goons were relatives of powerful men. The police would be better off saving such criminals than by taking them to task. All this in a democracy by the people, of the people for the people. Are we turning into a nation of goons? pondered Ayan.

As Kashmira's truck rolled on, Ayan read what was written behind his vehicle.

NANAK NAAM
CHARHDI KALAN
TERE BAHANE SUB DA BHALA

(Nanak asks for 'Naam' (name of God) with which comes well-being, happiness and positive spirit. With your blessings, Lord, may everyone in the world prosper and be in peace).

Ayan drove to a small medical store a few kilometres away and got the petrified girl's wounds on her hands cleaned up, medicated and bandaged. He dropped the sobbing girl a short distance from her home as per her request. 'Will you tell your parents about what happened?' asked Ayan.

'No Sir. I will say there was a small accident. My parents are very poor. Thank you.'

After the ordeal, Ayan went for a run in a nearby park in the evening. He needed to forget the experience of the morning. He ran for thirty minutes. He did not enjoy the exercise as the air seemed a bit suffocating. The Delhi air was quite polluted. As he came out of the park, the road was choked with traffic. People, after a whole day's work were driving back home in cars, two wheelers, buses. Their faces were tired, irritated and impatient to reach home. I wonder how they will behave with their wives, children or elder dependents at home. Maybe they would find electricity failure, maids not come to clean utensils, homework problems for kids, wife suffering a viral infection. Life is tough in India for so many people, thought Ayan.

As Ayan was thinking of all such things, walking towards the parking area, he stopped to observe a fascinating scene. Under a flyover, a lady, perhaps from a migrant labour family was making *chappatis*. A small fire was burning. On a shrivelled old aluminium plate lay a lump of kneaded *atta*. Over the fire, in a small utensil, *dal* was being boiled. Next to the utensil, on the fire was a round steel pan. There was an improvised tong with which the lady was turning over the round flattened *atta* and making *chappatis*. Nearby there was an improvised hummock made of dirty cloth, fixed by ropes and two iron rods. In the hummock was a small, perhaps a one-year-old baby, sleeping peacefully amidst all the noise and dust generated by the sea of traffic on the roads. Off and on, the lady attended to the boiling *dal*, the baking *chappatis* and swinging the hammock so that the child slept on. She was humming a rural song to herself. Three more children under the flyover were playing with a plastic ball. She was keeping an eye on them so that they did not stray towards the road. As she made the *chappatis*, she gave one to a dog sitting nearby, watching her intently. Even within her limited means, she was feeding the stray dog. The dog gobbled up the food and went towards a pit of sand. One child was playing with the sand trying to make a fort. He was also talking to the dog about what he was trying to construct. The dog was intently looking at him with alert ears, wagging its tail, as if it understood the conversation. The lady was chatting with this child occasionally.

My God, this is some multitasking, undertaken by this poor lady! Yet she seemed happy, contented, quite resigned to her destiny. The fact that she was able to feed her children and have free accommodation under the flyover in a big city made her feel better. Perhaps it was much worse in her rural village in Bihar or Rajasthan or wherever. Nearby, there was a glittering mall and many expensive eating places. How on earth could one describe the contradictions in this massive entity of India? wondered Ayan pensively.

He noticed a graveyard across the road. It was a serene place indeed. He pondered to himself. The dead there are lucky indeed, to be buried in the greenest part of the highly polluted city, the urban jungle of Delhi. He prayed in his mind. 'God help those who are in a position to govern well and improve India. May God grant them intellectual spines and moral testicles. They must nurture genuine love and devotion for this nation. Patriotism in India needs to be redefined in such terms rather than in slogans and chanting.' When wrong people with different agendas and motives take on the onerous task of defining patriotism in India, it seems akin to allowing the devil to define divinity and humanity, thought Ayan.

Suddenly, it started raining. Ayan stood under the canopy of a big neem tree. He watched with amazement as a bunch of urchins started dancing, laughing, singing some rural songs as they soaked in the rain drops. The steady beat of the rainfall acted like a symphony orchestra for them. Their dirty faces glowed. They were feeling a sense of freedom and emancipation from the oppressive summer heat. Their faces looked beautiful as those of happy children do. They were enjoying the shower of the first pre-monsoon rains after a painful wait of over three months. Ayan rued the fact that these children would never go to school in their lives.

He steadily watched the scene. A girl came out of the shelter of a plastic sheet. This was her home at this point in time. She looked up at the sky with deep gratitude and wet herself with the bountiful raindrops. Then suddenly she pondered awhile. She went in and brought out a few old plastic buckets. She wanted to harvest the clean rain water with all the storing capacity she had.

Suddenly Ayan remembered Rabindranath Tagore, 'Where the mind is without fear and the head is held high, where knowledge is free, where the world has not been broken up into fragments by narrow domestic walls…where the mind is led forward by thee, into every widening thought and action, into that heaven of freedom, my father, let my country awake.'

Ayan joined a major logistical company in Prague. He was happy with his campus placement from the Singapore Management Academy. During the job interview, he was glad to note that the HR department of the employing company was quite happy to have selected him. The thought of going to work in Prague amidst a European environment pleased him. He had no interest in getting a job and starting his professional career in India. Later perhaps, he pondered. He gave himself up to ten years to learn, imbibe and hone his professional growth in a global environment. There was so much to learn in an environment of better management techniques, work ethos and superior leadership practices.

As the Czech Air aircraft hovered over Prague, Ayan looked outside and held his breath. Wow! What a beautiful creation of a city. He could see a lovely river dominating the fascinating landscape. The air hostess smiled and bending down told him, 'That is the Vitava River. That castle you see is the Prague Castle, the biggest ancient castle in the world.' She spoke softly as if to a friend, as she rushed on to get seated herself before the landing, leaving behind a sweet lavender smell. Ayan could not locate the castle due to such a lovely distraction. In fact, throughout the flight, the behaviour of the staff was no nice, so natural and so polite. It is a beautiful country indeed, with its graceful, charming people, he thought.

Ayan saw the efficiency, the no nonsense yet polite attitude of everyone at the airport including the immigration officials. These officers appeared conscious of the fact that they were the first people the incoming passengers would encounter to form their initial opinion of the country. How much one can learn by such global exposure? lamented Ayan, thinking about Mumbai and Delhi International Airports.

He came out of gate No 10 as directed by the HR guy in the welcome mail. A smiling young man held a small placard bearing his name. Ayan smiled, mockingly stood at attention and gave him a salute, 'Ayan reporting Sir. You must be Nick.'

Nick laughed aloud and warmly shook his hand. 'Welcome to Prague, Ayan, and welcome to my team of four. Your joining us will enrich our team. For the first three weeks you will stay in a hotel. By then, we will organise some accommodation for you. For three weeks your stay will be complimentary from our Company.'

Nick clicked a quick message on his mobile. They had walked a few hundred metres or so when a car smoothly drove up next to them. A smartly dressed man came out and took charge of the luggage and welcomed Ayan to Prague with a warm, firm handshake. Nice feeling on arrival. Everything so organised, cool and so naturally efficient, thought Ayan to himself.

He relaxed and got over his jet lag by next morning. The hotel was great. Services were perfect. Everything was spick and span. Exactly at 9 am Nick arrived at the reception. Both came out of the hotel, walked for ten minutes to a bus stop. Exactly at 9.15 am, Bus No 17 cruised in which took them to the main street. It took twenty-five minutes to reach their destination. Having alighted, they crossed the street and after a fifteen minute walk reached the office complex.

'So, you are assured of the benefits of fifty minutes of walking every day from the hotel to the work place. There is a small gym in our office complex where we work out every day. In our type of work, we need to exercise to remain fit. Moreover, Czech ladies do not bother about guys who are not slim and healthy, my friend,' teased Nick with a grin.

As they entered the office, Ayan noticed that the entire environment was mesmerisingly calm, quiet and intense. People were working with great concentration and keenness. When two people working together wanted to discuss something, it would be done very softly without disturbing the others. The work cubicles were smartly designed.

Nick took Ayan to the office of the Senior Manager, Mr Johnson. As they walked towards his office, Nick mentioned, 'Ayan, Boss is a very dynamic and competent person. Besides, he has big heart. Intolerant of careless, listless performance, he is otherwise a buddy to the core. He is known for his strategic insight and a gut feeling like that of a trained commando. He served in an infantry battalion in the dangerous Helmand province of Afghanistan for a year of voluntary attachment. He has a soft corner for the military.'

Ayan gratefully absorbed this input about his first boss.

As Ayan was ushered into the office, Nick came out. Mr Johnson strode out of his chair and gave him a warm handshake. He looked at him smilingly, but with deep intensity and took him towards the chair in front of his desk. Ayan was taken aback by such a display of humility. Indian bosses would hardly behave so informally.

'Welcome to Prague, Ayan, to one of the biggest logistic enterprises in the world, though we do have a couple of capable global competitors.'

'Thank you, Sir,' replied Ayan.

'No need of the term 'Sir'. Here we address each other by first name. Our terms of engagement are based on comradeship, commitment and complete team spirit. It just so happens that due to more years of experience, eight years in our case, I am in charge of the team,' said Mr Johnson smiling, as they both sat down. 'We value the power of 'we' over 'I', the power of teamwork and mutual trust. Now Ayan, your resume was interesting to read. You first ventured into the Merchant Navy. You saw the world. It must have been a tough experience. Historically, sailors have been the tough ones. The sea as well as the ship are unforgiving in their handling. Sailing is akin to soldiering. I also noted that your dad served in the army for his entire professional life. In which branch of the army did he serve?'

'He was in the infantry, "the queen of battle", as he always used to insist on calling it,' replied Ayan.

'Absolutely true,' nodded Mr Johnson. 'Have you noticed the fact that practically all nations of today's developed world enforced compulsory military training for its citizens till the Second World War? Of course, that was due to the circumstances of the earlier centuries. But see the demographic dividend they possessed due to nationwide military training. Look at the sense of discipline, the spirit of obedience to existing laws and regulations, the desire to be productive, creative and the pride for the nation that exists in the developed world. Great Britain, in fact, went about manufacturing products to sustain the wars with great military precision. If that spirit can be maintained when there are no major wars, then any nation can become prosperous and productive. Therefore, military ethos and business world are mutually complimentary.'

'True,' responded Ayan, now comfortable with the way his first meeting with his first boss in professional life was shaping.

'Okay Ayan, settle down in the work environment. We shall have enough opportunities to talk shop about the nuts and bolts of our project. Nick will put you through the paces. I am confident that your joining us will create a more diverse, dynamic team, with greater variety of perspectives. Together we shall work hard relentlessly, cheerfully, from Mondays to Fridays.'

Nick smiled as Ayan came out of Mr Johnson's office.

'He is a fine soul as well as a hard taskmaster. He will get the best out of you, make no mistake about that. Under him, you will realise how much hard work you are capable of. The beauty is that you will rarely feel the pressure of work. At times when you do, you will always feel that he is aware of it and appreciates it.'

Sneha at Cambridge University

> 'Spreading the jam will be a social revolution which will make the world more peaceful'–(Sneha in Cambridge)

Sneha was quite overwhelmed by the superb academic environment of the vast expanse called The University of Cambridge. Oh God! Thank you for facilitating my coming here. Goddess Saraswati resides in every nook and corner of this centre of learning, she said to herself.

On a pleasant Saturday afternoon, she walked along the famous River Cam, which meandered through the university. Each side of the river was like an immaculate golf course, interspersed with various colleges with beautiful green lawns. First came the beautiful areas called Coe Fen and Sheep's Green. The Department of Engineering lay to her right and a short distance to her left she saw the sprawling Darwin College, then Queen's college, King's College. She noticed the Cambridge University Library to her left. She walked along towards Trinity Hall, Clare

College and Trinity College to her right. Everything was picture perfect. The entire environment was academic, serene and full of quiet efficiency. Groups of students squatted on the greens. Practically every girl student had some book or reading material in her hands. Most of the young gentlemen students had beverage bottles, cans or snack packets in their hands. Everyone looked happy and intelligent. Along the river were similar groups on boats, paddling away, laughing, chatting and singing. One such boat was full of Indian students singing Bollywood songs. Finally, she returned to her room around the premises of Wolfson College.

Mrs Mary Chick was Sneha's guide. She was as pretty as a doll despite her middle age. Always immaculately dressed, her impeccable behaviour, great depth of knowledge and analytical mind was very inspirational indeed. She insisted that she be addressed by her first name. Sneha's first interaction with Mary was extremely informal and comradely. Sneha was impressed by her behaviour and poise.

'Sneha, please consider that I am also a participant in your research. We will learn a lot from each other. I have always been very impressed with research students from India. The lady researchers particularly have displayed stunning academic calibre, as well as personal attributes. So, here is how we start our long journey in the knowledge train together. You organise your thoughts, reflections on the subject of your study. Research, read up and gobble up as much as you can from our library and elsewhere. You can write down your random thoughts as they come to you. As and when you feel like, you can show them to me. I shall then call you in and we will have a discourse. Will that be okay with you, Sneha?'

'Yes'. Sneha still hesitated to call Mary by her first name. 'When should I start?'

'Oh take your time. As you flow with your train of thoughts, you will reach a thought block when you will come to a mental dead end. That will be the time when you summarise and organise your ideas and thoughts. Come to me then. It will keep happening, so do not feel bad. That is how it will be, it should be. Please also be free to share your personal space, whenever you need to do so. If any personal matter is bothering you, do come and share your worries with me. I fully understand how a young lady feels when so far away from family, particularly the mother. You will recollect the fights you had with your mom as you were growing up. I still do. Somehow, we daughters do this more than our brothers. You will at times think of those incidents as they flash through your mind and cry. Don't worry. Cry out and you will feel lighter. Do not feel guilty. It is natural. Our moms are the most divine, forgiving creators on earth. So will we be, as we move on in life. Our children will be the centre of gravity of our lives. This is life. You Indian ladies are far more committed to emotions and relationships. We all here are a family, a global family pursuing knowledge together. Remember and feel the fact that you are studying in the best university of the world.'

Sneha lay down on the bed of her small but adequate room. Below on the ground floor was a well-equipped kitchen provided for each group of students. One could keep eggs, bread, butter etc. in the large refrigerator. No one touched the stuff of another normally. If somebody took an egg, he or she would inform the owner. The item was later replaced. Borrowing was a normal process. Stealing hardly took place. Wherever it took place, it was invariably be a boy who had done it. It was in banter and fun as the guy would confess soon enough.

She felt better and more relaxed each day. The Chinese students were the best behaved, meticulous in abiding by the set rules and norms. Their food habits were rather apart from the others. However, they appeared proud to be Chinese and of their potential. Europeans were nice, though initially a bit formal. Americans were a jovial lot, serious only during studies.

Japanese students were very friendly during direct interactions but otherwise quite serious in their demeanour while working.

Indian students—well they were their usual selves, chatterboxes, but pretty efficient in their studies. Generally they were more nostalgic about their country and lamented about the lack of development, infrastructure, the prevailing quality of politicians and bureaucrats in particular, and moral, ethical bankruptcy in general. Coming into environments such as Cambridge University, they felt that their capabilities and energies were released from the chains and shackles, which had held them back in India. They felt like bonsai plants taken out of the confines of their pots and replanted on fertile grounds, free to grow to their true potential. They felt like birds released from cages, free to fly with the sky as the limit. They also realised that they had all reasons to be proud to be Indian as their academic potential was second to none, even in the best competitive global environment.

Sneha started writing down her thoughts on the subject of 'Skill Development And Employment Generation', based on wide reading on this issue. She thought it best to start with what she studied about this during the Industrial Revolution in the West, in 1760s to about 1840s.

'The process of industrial revolution was essentially a mammoth shift to new modes of manufacturing. This was the shift from existing methods of hand- made production, to use of new machines and technology to produce goods on a massive scale. Therefore, goods of all types—from metal production, processers, chemicals, methods relating to increasing water power, steam power, machine tools to leaner labour efficiencies were taking place. It was really a very revolutionary method of transition in the process of human growth. Industrial revolution, like any other revolution marked a turning point in history, influencing almost every aspect of daily life. It also created turbulence in society just as any other revolution.

'It began in Great Britain and spread to Western Europe and North America within a few decades. The first Industrial Revolution evolved into the second Industrial Revolution between 1840 and 1870 with steam transport, railways, boats and ships, large scale manufacturing of machine tools etc. Such a massive manufacturing venture was not possible without providing multi-level skills to workers. Thus, began the concept of apprenticeship training in places of production, the factories. Apprenticeship training ensured up-gradation of skills under a legal agreement, that defines the duration and conditions of relationship between the master, the corporate business enterprises and the apprentices. Therefore, the corporate world has to be the major stakeholder in the enterprise along with the government.

'There were far more unskilled labourers who would work for any price. Many of the unemployed or underemployed skilled workers such as hand weavers, whose talents became useless due to arrival of textile machines, were reduced to starvation. Such formerly skilled workers who earned twenty to thirty shillings per week were now compelled to live on five shillings despite working for ten to fourteen hours per day. Hazards like polluting air, diseases and accidents took their toll. The first generation of workers suffered immensely. Child labour was rampant. Gradually a middle class level of workers started emerging . From 1790 to 1850, the life of workers hardly improved.

'In the earliest times in Egypt and Babylon too, training in crafts and skills was organised in order to maintain adequate numbers of skilled workers. The Code of Hammurabi of Babylon which dates from eighteenth century BCE, required artisans to teach their crafts to the next generation.

'By thirteenth century, a similar practice emerged in Europe, in the form of Craft Guilds. Guild members supervised the quality of products, methods of production, and work conditions of a group of workers in every town. In 1563, to prevent exploitation of craftsmen, the condition of apprenticeship with statutes of Artificers was started.

'The Industrial revolution altered attitudes towards skill training. Machines created the need for both skilled and unskilled workers. The unskilled employees who displayed aptitudes advanced to some skilled jobs; apprenticeship training grew in importance with the development of trade unions. It is worthwhile to note that Benjamin Franklin, the future President of America served as an apprentice to his brother in a printing trade.

'As the demand for workers with specialised skills grew due to demand for manufactured goods, the workers grew ambitious to graduate to better skills. Such was the revolution. So training institutes were established through which jobs were available during 1820s to 1860s.

'When workers get skilled, their productivity increases as does their bargaining power with their neo-rich employees who are major beneficiaries of any manufacturing revolution. In India, such a working class maybe around 70 per cent of the society. This includes practically all of the rural and some urban constituents of its demographic dividend.'

Sneha continued writing and penned her thoughts based on what she had read.

'You get dividend only when you invest wisely. You harvest only when you grow good crops. Skill development is the investment from which dividend will accrue. Otherwise, hundreds of millions of youth, without hope, can at best become terrorists or criminals. They will be part of the seamless numbers of penniless humans with no country to call their own. This will cause a demographic disaster—a devastating revolution of chaotic proportions. Youthquake can do more damage than an enormous earthquake.'

Sneha stopped writing, got up and walked around the room pensively. She was in deep thought. After a few minutes she sat down and started writing again as thoughts came into her mind.

'Without a well-conceived, coordinated national plan backed by international support, a nation of such vastness as India cannot implement such a complex endeavour of skill training and apprenticeship training. Looking at India's bad record in efficient implementation of grandiose plans, conceived by white collared bureaucrats, one tends to be sceptical. India's ability to deliver good governance, its unabashed and no holds barred corruption at all levels is very much of the third world. India has to break through these shackles to tackle skill training and apprenticeship on a war footing. Well over 30 per cent of India's massive population of over one billion people is in the gutter of poverty.'

Sneha wrote her heart out and felt tired. She went down to the kitchen. She opened the refrigerator, took out her coffee powder and milk pack and made herself a strong mug of coffee. As she came back to her room she wondered whether it was a correct approach to make the Industrial Revolution of the West from 1760s to 1840s, her starting point.

She decided to relax by going on a Skype-chat with her mom and dad. It was such fun chatting with dad and teasing mom a bit. Wonder how Govind is doing? she thought. Sneha felt fresh and energised after chatting with her parents. She wrote on…

'How on earth could a country be an emerging super power if its major segments of rural communities lack the ability to feed, clothe, house, and raise productive children? The poor will view the rich as carnivorous animals with an insatiable hunger for more for themselves. The resultant conflict will be terrible. Among multipronged means of preventing this collapse, skill training, associated job generation to sustain a massive economic growth, is one of the critical needs.

'The unskilled, semi-skilled, badly skilled and hence less productive people comprise a big part of humanity. They will be left out of the globalisation process. They will be part of twenty-first century slaves. Economic slavery will face grave injustices. India has shown tremendous, world class potential in space technology, nuclear science, economics and business management. Boys and girls from malnourished families have won medals in athletics, wrestling, hockey, boxing and shooting against far better trained and fed players from developed countries. So there is hope.

'Politicians in third world countries use a big word like Poverty Eradication, while being insensitive in commitment towards the poor. We must first try to make poverty a little less painful. It also has to be made less permanent.'

Sneha looked out of the window at the lovely view outside, and continued writing.

'Creation of more jobs, skills and direct enabling assistance is needed. People have to be moved from non-opportunity areas to areas that need more workers. It is about rehabilitation and resettlement based on the skills training given to them formally. One sees the way people from Eritrea, Nigeria, Syria, Iraq etc. are running away from the murdering extremists, just to live, to save their women and children. When I see them, I feel that, we, the better off people have just won the birth lottery. We have been lucky to have been born in a relatively better and sane part of geography.'

Sneha pondered, biting the end of her ball pen. She put on some soft music. She loved the soothing effect of Lang Lang's piano tunes. He was really a great pianist and he looked so cute. His smile not only emanated from his lips but was also reflected in his eyes. Wasn't he handsome? What immense talent? The divine effect of the music made her mind more awake, more alert. She started the last bit of writing for this session.

'The construction Industry has been one of the largest contributors of GDP in India. Yet, it faces the biggest challenge of an unskilled workforce. In developed countries, the skilled workforce is between 60 per cent and 90 per cent of total workforce. India has only 5 per cent of its massive workforce who are skilled with formal vocational training. How can India execute its 'Make in India' strategy? How can India become the world's skill capital as envisioned unless it undertakes massive skill development projects? The present Prime Minister of India is spot on in realising this.

'The construction sector itself will require over 30 million skilled workers by 2022. Overall, a hundred million people in India itself need to be trained for floor tiling, bricklaying, masonry, stone-casting, plumbing, wood-work and electrical works. Many more are needed to handle machines, maintain the equipment, painting, repair work—the list is endless. Such massive training has to be outcome based, conducted by professionals and in the private sectors too, as part of corporate social responsibility. It is too vast, too critical to be left to politicians and autocratic rulers of nations. The civilised world and those who wield power have to conduct this twenty-first century revolution in human affairs to ensure a better world for over billions of growing numbers of humanity.'

Sneha felt that India needed dozens of Bill Gates who would create an environment of the 'Giving Pledge', where rich donate huge chunks of their fortunes to productive charity. Skill development of the poor is the mother of all charities.

'Why should we invest in skill training projects? Investment is postponed consumption. Usually our brains are hardwired for current consumption. This aspect should be taught in all Management Institutions in greater depth. Professor Walter Mischel's famous term called Marshmellow Test is worth knowing. He taught children about postponed consumption.

He rewarded children with two sweets if they could defer the pleasure of eating the first sweet. Through this simple test or rather a game he taught them that we should not lose sight of the need for future assurance, without having to earn it later.

'So the Marshmellow Test drives home the point that investment is not an end in itself, but a means to an end. The end is assuring the future by postponing a bit of consumption or profits now. This requires self restraint.'

Sneha was tired from her efforts. Not a bad way to start the thinking process amidst the excellent academic environment of Cambridge University, she pondered. Mary Chick will be satisfied with my thoughts on this subject, I guess. When we meet during my first session with her, she will add more value, which will put me on a higher threshold on the subject, yawned Sneha closing her notes.

Naveen in Singapore

Naveen settled down in his job at Singapore. He joined a construction company as a Senior Engineer. The pay was comfortable while work schedule was pretty intense. Singapore was quite a great place as far as work culture was concerned.

The biggest attraction of Singapore was the unique blending of its rich tapestry of culture into a harmonious whole. In terms of religious tolerance, Singapore is a multi-religion mosaic with beautifully constructed and preserved diverse places of worship. The majestic Armenian Church is an architectural masterpiece. The Buddha Tooth Relic Temple and Museum is a Tang styled Chinese Buddhist Temple in Chinatown. The Chinatown Heritage Centre depicts how Chinese migrants in the past lived here. The Eurasian Heritage Centre depicts the history and culture of Eurasian community in Singapore. Similarly, the Fuk Tak Chi Museum, Sri Mariamman Temple, the Jama-Ath Mosque are splendid. Everywhere one sees the mosaic of Chinese, Malay, Indian, Urasian and Perankar cultures.

The business culture is equally fascinating. In most cases, as a foreigner, one is likely to encounter a Singaporean Chinese as a business counterpart, as they form the majority of the population. So, one is expected to adapt to their business culture. Local customs have great influence on their business style.

They are generally open and cosmopolitan in their overall outlook. They expect you to follow the dictum, to do there as the Singaporeans do. You are expected to be very tolerant and sensitive to all cultures existing in Singapore. To be civilized is to observe all rules, regulations, laws and expected mode of behaviour. To do this is no problem. It only requires you to be considerate. One must avoid discussing religious, social issues and politics. English is the working language. Locally it is Singlish which essentially is English laced with local expressions. Punctuality is the norm.

Singaporeans are open hearted to all outsiders provided that they feel you respect them and their culture too. Though they are not flamboyant in showing off, they are significantly more capable and knowledgeable, than what foreigners tend to give them credit for. With them there is no scope for arrogance and insensitivity. They look forward to greater experience levels, strategic and leadership capabilities from foreigners, which would add to the betterment of Singapore.

It is a very sophisticated, cultured society, where people are very well educated and the pace of development and change is phenomenal. Their education system is world class. They expect greater cross cultural understanding and mutual respect. They do not waste time in discussing petty issues and dogmas.

Singapore is the ideal country in the world for genuine blending of East and West, based on equality and civilized behaviour. Its philosophy is the best foundation on which to build the rise of Asia in the twenty-first century for global benefit, relative peace and co-prosperity.

Naveen's parents were settled in Belgaum, Karnataka. Belgaum is essentially a small town with a prominent military cantonment established for the training of junior officers of the Indian army by the British. Naveen's father retired from the army as an officer with a distinguished service in the Corps of Artillery. Since retirement, after completing his Masters in Business Management, he worked as a Director in an MBA Institute in Pune for fifteen years. Just like Ayan's parents, they too were not too comfortable with Naveen's choice of Merchant Navy as a career.

'If you wish to sail, you might as well join the elite Indian Navy. You will lead a smart, adventurous life as a naval officer. It will be a high quality career full of dignity and elan. If you do well, then in your batch you may be come an Admiral. That will be great, though only a very few will be Admirals. If you don't, then you can serve till you are fifty-six years old, and then you can join the merchant navy if you so wish for a few more years to earn some money. Military life will not make you rich by civilian standards,' his father told Naveen.

Naveen had responded, 'Dad, I have seen you facing so much financial hardship while educating your children well. Haven't we gone through that? Yes, you lived a life of adventure and dignity, but you and maa were always struggling to make ends meet. When you had to retire at the age of fifty-six because vacancies beyond the rank of the Colonel were too few, we know what you went through. Your pension was far less and you were under great stress. You were forced to sell the flat in Pune to manage your commitments. If you had kept that flat you would have been so much more comfortable.

'The Army ensured that you remained proud of your profession and made you feel honoured. What did the nation do for you? The nation kept you underpaid and deprived you of your rightful benefits and dues. Had you joined Central

Civil Services, Railways, even State Civil Services, you would have been financially so much more comfortable. Seeing your condition, I had decided not to join the army. However, I have seen the military profession since childhood and I feel that it is truly the most honourable profession in Indian society. I have often wondered if India deserves to have such an army, though it surely needs it. So please dad, let us not discuss this aspect further.'

'Okay *mere baap*! Go sail the high seas. Keep your mind open about what you want to do eventually. The world is large, beyond the seas,' replied his dad smiling.

Finally, after a four year stint in Merchant Navy as an engineer, Naveen met Ayan in Mumbai. They both decided that though nothing was wrong with pursuing this career, they were not suited to this type of life as individuals. They were already in touch with each other on this matter. It was providential that both got admission in Singapore for an MBA. Their destiny seemed to be interlinked.

Both had spent their childhood in military cantonments of India. Both had deep respect for the military profession and would forever be wedded to it. But both were clear in their minds not to pursue it as their profession. This was the second decade of the twenty-first century and many of this generation were a globalised lot. Their urge was to explore beyond the boundaries of India, into the more developed regions of the world. The sky was their limit. They also wanted to prove to the developed world that India had enormous talent and capabilities. They only needed to be enabled to display their potential. Such an enabling environment was more readily available out of the confines of India. This generation of Asian youth were more daring, confident to prove their worth. Their horizon of perspectives, vision, was limitless. They were not constrained by narrow issues of religion, caste, polities and other disempowering thoughts.

However, they were deeply patriotic, though critical of the state of affairs of their countries.

Just as Buddhism grew bigger when it left India, this twenty-first generation of young Indians were leaving India to become global. They would further the interests of India from outside.

Naveen's boss and Managing Director was Colonel (retired) Tang. He had been in the Singapore army. Colonel, as he was addressed in day to day interactions, was an ex-para artillery officer. He was a motivator and an effective leader. He hardly displayed white collar attitudes, except when he was formally interacting in board meetings and tours abroad. He enjoyed being in touch with line workers, managers and the teams; and spent as much time as he could with them. When the Colonel was among them, he displayed tremendous energy and happiness. All in all, he was a typical military man. Over a glass of beer with his subordinates he would say, 'I am unmarried and pathologically self contained,' with a loud laugh. Every time he would repeat this sentence he would laugh aloud. Then he would add, 'If I had married, I would have been a '*wasband*' rather a husband very soon.'

In one chat he had with his department he had mentioned, 'When you are young, spend time with older people to get wise. In our profession anyone whose job experience is a decade plus more than yours is old. Then spend time with younger people to learn innovations and new concepts. So, I expect such innovations, new ideas and good outcomes from you all. My job is to enjoy the pleasure of being your leader and pass on whatever wisdom, experiences I have had, to you all. The show is mainly yours. I can only assure you that I shall not be a pain in the arse! In the army the critical common denominator is the soldier. Any army is only as good as its soldiers. You all are corporate soldiers, Lieutenants, Captains and Majors. So, carry on regardless. Your generation is open to new ideas, willing to stretch and willing to relocate. A mix of two to three generations lends itself to broader and more dynamic working environments. I am here to help you do your best.'

Col Tang was a phenomenal person. He had worked with quite a few multinational companies. Each of these companies would look forward to his rejoining any time. Such was his reputation. His military background was very dear to him. Every company he worked for was like his Regiment. The interests, welfare and progress of his Regiment was supreme. If any boss of the Colonel was not sensitive to the interest of his Regiment, he would say so politely but firmly with no other biases or prejudices. He would never criticise his boss in front of others but only do so in the privacy of his office. Most of the time, his sincerity of purpose would prevail on the boss. There were times when an equally efficient boss would convince him on some issues. He would unhesitatingly accept his view point and invite him for a drink in the evening as an acknowledgement. Whenever mistakes were made by his group, he would, like a typical military leader take the blame on himself and sort out the problem but give credit his subordinates when things were done well.

Colonel Tang had been nominated while he was in service by the Singapore army to attend the National Defence College Course in New Delhi. It was a year long course. He had spent a sabbatical year learning larger aspects of National Security paradigm. He had made many friends among the Indian military officers, and understood their sentimental attachment towards their country and respect for democracy. As part of the curriculum, he had visited the states of Tamil Nadu and Punjab for a week each. The course content was laced with visits to border regions, industrial complexes and foreign tours. Colonel Tang was very nostalgic about this experience indeed.

'We saw so many shades of Indian panorama. It was an

amazing experience, though very perplexing in many contexts. It is a nation where all religions of the world are trying hard to coexist. In India's success in such coexistence lies the hope of global coexistence. It is a country of so much unrealised capabilities and talent. A country of such porous and serious historical fault lines, where hope and despair cohabitate so delicately. A country which is urgently in need of good governance and leaders of stature and vision,' he exclaimed to Naveen.

Naveen was returning from Hong Kong to Singapore. He was nominated to attend a two day seminar on the theme 'Will the twenty-first Century be an Asian Century? A Realistic Assessment, Transcending Nationalistic Fervour.' Naveen sat in an aisle seat of the Air China craft and reflected on the awesome experience he had gained while attending the global seminar. He was thankful to his company for financing his tour and giving him such an exposure.

During the seminar, the keynote speaker spoke in such a forthright and candid manner, with a display of intellectual honesty, despite being from China. Naveen recollected the contents of his address from the elaborate notes he had made. He was a young CEO of a flourishing Chinese business firm.

> 'Ladies and Gentleman, the rise of Asia will not be an East versus West phenomena, as is commonly assumed by those who have intellectual deficiencies. Just as erosion of Asia does not result in rise of the West, erosion of the West does not auger well for the prospects of rise of Asia. However, it may well be that rivalries within Asian countries will go counter to the idea of an Asian sunrise. The challenge is in managing Asian fault lines.
>
> 'For the last three decades China has been leading global growth. The West perceives it as the world's most populated nation in the Asian continent and its huge growth as the leader of Asian continent, reasserting itself after 250 years

of foreign aggression, oppression and humiliation. The world also talks about Napoleon's futuristic, prescient and ominous caution about rise of China. Nevertheless, it is too simplistic and unreal an assumption that Pan Asian solidarity, predominated by China will oppose the western world as Soviet Union did earlier.

'Asia is not Europe. Europe is a very small entity. Asia is too vast in size. Apart from its vast geographical size, there are diverse cultures, religions, varying economic conditions, demographics, ideologies, social characteristics and fierce sense of identities.

'Therefore, the first requirement to my mind is to Ideate a strong, united Asia, its vision, its core concept. It has to be conceived and choreographed by involving Asia's fourth and fifth generations. They must be the stakeholders and must be involved, not only leaders above sixty years of age.

'A few words about Chinese younger generation today. The country's opening to the West has allowed millions of Chinese citizens to satisfy their curiosity about the developed world. More Chinese tourists are travelling the world than the combined population of many Western nations. Such exposures have not fuelled restlessness among the young generation. They have understood the advantage of globalisation and the benefits that accrue to them without the need for any radical change in China.

'One child policy of China was instituted in 1978. Today China has a whole generation of young people, who are single children. They are obsessed with consumerism, internet, video games and inviting goods from all over the world to be sent to China along with related services. China has not only changed itself, but changed the developed world. Now it will change Asia. To do this, China has to develop the culture of shared leadership with other Asian nations and the ASEAN. This will be a critical enigma of the twenty-first century.

'So, will economic growth eventually bring democracy to China? Young Chinese do not seem to be excited by this prospect. I wonder if the West should plan on such a development in China. Economic progress is above democracy and that is how it shall be. It is decoupled from democracy. The young generation, proud of China's achievements will brook no actions or agitations, which will tarnish the present reality of a powerful China. So, the economic progress of China must roll on, enriching regions of Asia as well as the developed world. Rise of Asia is inclusive to the peaceful rise of China.'

Naveen's thoughts were disrupted by a radiantly smiling, dignified Chinese airhostess. He asked for coffee. She was pretty and efficient. Naveen felt that the Chinese always displayed the attitude of being very work oriented and focused. The way they carried themselves, their gait and persona reflected this. They were correct, at times clinically so in their behaviour. They had a natural penchant for obeying rules, regulations and were always guarded in their private space. Perhaps they thought deep and talked less creating a mystique about themselves.

As far as fellow Asians were concerned, the Chinese appeared to know them rather well, particularly Indians. They had been studying India for centuries by sending their people here. It suddenly struck Naveen that instead of Napoleon, so far away in France, it should have been an Indian Emperor or a strategic thinker who could have cautioned India about a sleeping China and the earth-shaking power it could be, when it awakened. China woke up in the 1970s. India continued to sleepwalk, with occasional delusional dreams about itself. Naveen and his generation of Indians had no doubt that when India awakened and upgraded its potential, China would make friends with

India. Not till then. Durable friendships are forged amongst equals or near equals.

As Naveen looked out of the window, he was greeted by a patch of clear blue sky with occasional groups of scattered clouds appearing now and then. How beautiful are the designs these small groups of clouds make at times. From Hong Kong to Thailand, Malaysia and Singapore, Asia looked similar in many aspects. The Chinese presence in most nations of Association of South East Asian Nations, ASEAN was prominent. It was also a stabilizing factor in Malaysia, Singapore, Thailand, Indonesia etc.

The overseas Chinese population had played a large role in the development of economies in the region. Their business communities were connected through a network of overseas business operators sharing common family and cultural ties. Their origins in these South East Asian countries could be traced back to the sixteenth century when Chinese migrants from Southern China settled in Indonesia, Thailand and other countries around. In the sixteenth century India, there were social taboos on leaving Indian shores. Chinese population in these regions saw a rapid increase following the Communist Revolution in 1949, forcing many refugees to immigrate out of China. Some thirty million Chinese lived in South East Asia. During the seminar in Hong Kong , a speaker highlighted the aspect of religion. He stated that Islam was the most widely practised religion in South East Asia, numbering about 40 per cent of the entire population, with majority in Brunei, Indonesia, Malaysia and in South Philippines.

Buddhism is predominant in Thailand, Cambodia, Laos, Myanmar, Vietnam and Singapore. Christianity is predominant in Philippines, eastern Indonesia, East Malaysia, and East Timor. Ancestor worship is widely practised, along with Confucianism in Vietnam and Singapore. Pockets of Hindu population can also be found in Singapore, Malaysia and Indonesia etc. Garuda, the Hindu phoenix who is the mount of Vishnu is a national symbol of both Thailand and Indonesia. In the Philippines, gold images of Garuda have been found. Other gold images of Hindu Gods have been found elsewhere in South East Asia. Some also practise animism in bits and pieces.

A very critical and exclusive aspect about the growth and spread of religions in South East Asia is generally not noticed by the rest of the world. The religions have grown and survived, with their own characteristics. They are not totally predominated by Middle East characteristics or South Asian characteristics. Tolerance is inbuilt into the environment. Any foreigner who goes to Malaysia, Singapore, Thailand, Indonesia, Philippines, does not feel the sting of extreme radicalism as a major concern.

Surprisingly, Naveen could not help noticing that during most of the seminar, the focus was more on South East Asia. However, Japan, China, Koreas and India figured adequately. South Asia as a region was relegated in their priorities. Perhaps the feeling was that South Asia would have to up its ante to join the rise of Asia, at least for the time being. However, this was not stated as such.

As the aircraft prepared to land, the panoramic view of the immaculate sprawl of Singapore with the cobalt blue sky looked divine indeed. Somehow, one always felt uplifted while arriving at Singapore.

Once the Colonel was invited as a speaker for a global seminar on 'Industry Military Interface—the Road Ahead'. He got a slot of fifteen minutes to speak. The seminar was held at *The Gateway* in Singapore. The Colonel ensured that the invite was extended to two of his team members. Naveen was one of them. The Colonel would miss no opportunity to groom his subordinates by giving them wider exposure. The military ethos was deeply embedded in him.

It was indeed an excellent seminar. When the Colonel's turn came, he strode towards the podium. He could not avoid walking with his typical military gait. Slim and smart, erect, despite his greying, semi-bald head, he appeared impressive. Some of the sentences he spoke got etched in Naveen's mind.

'In business management, the boss says "you will". In the army, the subordinate says "I will". What does the army do? It defines objectives, sets clear overall parameters, trains itself consistently and lets the energetic, motivated subordinates decide how best to accomplish tasks. Subordinates come up with their own ideas and plans. The tactical plan is left to the people on the ground. They are challenged to plan and execute the missions, giving them autonomy, independence and trust. Doesn't all this sound like the culture we want to create for our business?

'The first thing that falls apart when enemy shelling starts is the original plan and that is when the dynamics of the situation dominate. Hereafter, it is all about motivation, leadership, small team efforts, innovations, improvisations and contingency plans. Small teams have unique capabilities, which high echelons of the organisations can never muster—trust and common purpose. They also have shared consciousness, empowered execution of doing the right things fast enough, with minimum resources. Shared consciousness is not what superiors think or the group thinks. It provides channels for diverse perspectives to be heard. The superior's views sometimes lead to faulty decisions.

'Just as the military believes in "Gods of War", there are also "Gods of Business War" too. Both are equally unpredictable. Military personnel live and breathe the value and importance of team work. They take responsibility, adapt to shifting priorities, the changes in focus and directions. No scope for looking backwards, though all possible logistics, technology, additional resources, fire power, always supports them from behind. The Leadership in military lies not only in front but, also in the rear. This must be understood and imbibed by the industry. Doesn't all this sound like the culture we all would like to create for our business?

'Ladies and gentleman, our flag does not fly because the wind moves it. It has always flown with the last breath of our soldiers who died protecting it. Our corporate flags fly due to the hard work of our corporate soldiers, duly backed from behind by corporate generals, many of whom are here in this seminar. The modern twenty-first century business leader must be an enabler who creates an enabling ecosystem for constant, never ending improvements. Elegant solutions in board rooms, however impressive will only succeed due to their execution by dynamic small teams in the field.

'Many business owners say that they want innovative, creative, collaborative, team oriented, motivated, spirited employees. Then, they lament that they cannot find those employees. They are there in the present younger generation. They are also available in the ex-military people and their children who have been brought up in military cantonments.

'Finally, Ladies and Gentleman, I have had the privilege of being nominated for a forty-seven week course as a Colonel to the National Defence College in India. As part of the curriculum, I visited the Ladakh region on the Himalayan border. I shall use slides to show you three boards displayed by the Indian Army.

"It is God's duty to forgive the enemy. Our duty is to convene a meeting between the two."

"What is a lifetime adventure for you here is a daily routine for us. (Ladakh-Leh Highway)."

"Either I will come back after hosting the national flag on the objective or I will be back wrapped in it, but I will be back for sure."

—Capt Vikram Batra
Param Veer Chakra (Posthumous)

'You may wonder why I have flashed these slides. I do so to highlight that we need such corporate soldiers, such spirit in our business world.

Radhika Meets Ziki Shaked in Israel

'Religion was invented when the con man met the first fool.'
—Mark Twain

Radhika felt rejuvenated after her tour of parts of Europe and Israel. During the tour she met many interesting people. She realised that deep down, human beings were fascinatingly similar, although they appeared to be so different in looks, colour, language, social environments, food habits, personal habits etc.

Radhika would always remember the unforgettable few days in Israel's southern port city of Eilat. It is on the Red Sea, near Jordan. Eilat is first mentioned in the Hebrew Bible, in the *Book of Exodus*. The first six stations of the Exodus are in Egypt. Seventh is the crossing of the Red Sea. The ninth to thirteenth are in and around Eilat. Eilat is located in the Gulf of Aqaba. It is recognised as one of the prime diving locations in the world. Radhika did a lot of scuba diving. It was here that she met Ziki Shaked, an Israeli girl approximately her age. Ziki was an astrophysicist in the University of Tel Aviv. Both of them also went on a fascinating camel tour. They became great friends. Somehow Radhika felt that for an Indian to make friends with someone in Israel was very easy, although no specific reason could be ascribed. One evening, Ziki offered to take her to a great restaurant in Eilat named *Rak Dagim*. This restaurant had perfect ambience and tasty food. They had two appetizers: an Israeli salad and roasted eggplant in tahini sauce, along with a sauvignon blanc. Then, Ziki suggested mussels in garlic cream sauce and then a red bream. It was divine.

People of Israel trace their origin to Abraham. As per Genesis 32:29, the name Israel derives from the name given to Jacob. His twelve sons were the kernels of twelve tribes that later developed into the Jewish nation. The name Jew derives from Yehuda, Judah, one of the twelve sons. The descendents of Abraham became a nation about 1300 BCE after their exodus from Egypt under the leadership of Moses. After forty years in the Sinai desert, Moses led them to the land of Israel—the land promised to the descendents of Abraham, Isaac and Jacob. Israel today is only forty miles wide even after four full scale wars with Arab states all around, Each was won decisively against an enemy many times more powerful than Israel.

Radhika spent a week with Ziki who took her from Eilat to Jerusalem and Tel Aviv and explained a lot of things about Israel. Radhika was fascinated. In Tel Aviv, Ziki took Radhika to a hundred year old winery, now converted into a pub. Over an excellent bottle of red wine they shared their thoughts, as childhood friends do.

Ziki explained Judaism to Radhika. She said, 'Judaism taught that God is omnipotent and omniscient. Yet Radhika, in reality, be it in relation to Israel or the world at large is that, it is dominated by much evil. So, we Jews particularly have the dilemma of reconciling the existence of this view about

God with the existence of evil all around. How can there be a God, with a devil around, who is always causing such misery to human beings? How can we, the modern Jews, have faith after the Holocaust? All our attitudes are influenced by prior experiences of such brutality meted to us. Are we forever cursed? If so, then we might as well die fighting back, so we never have to go through it all again.

'Radhika, the Arab-Israeli animosity is like a poison, embedded deep in the collective subconscious. It is our inheritance. It will continue to linger like all curses do. It will mutate in different ways. History and existentialism per se demand that we all have to be on guard forever. This is a cross we have to carry forever. All human systems carry the seeds of their own destruction. This is our share of it.'

Ziki continued, 'This is the land of vision as well as illusion. The vision for us Israelis is that Israel exists as an achieved aim. Our vision is of existence here, based on analysis of challenges, opportunities, risk assessment and national aim. For our enemies surrounding our little nation from three directions with the Mediterranean on the fourth side there is the illusion of killing all Jews in this country. Such is the immediate world around Israel. Western countries have a long history of getting along with evil regimes for their own need and greed. While doing so, they talk eloquently about human rights abuses when it suits them.

'You know Radhika, we Israelis will never have the luxury of normalcy or luxury of getting tired of war. Are we cursed since Biblical days? Will we ever be able to discover the wonders of existence?'

Radhika was quiet. She wanted Ziki to unload her emotions. After a small pause, Ziki continued, 'What sort of parents, grandparents were those who caused the world wars, slavery, the ruthless colonisation. What sort of humans were they who considered the helpless children and women as booty of war?

How did they bring up their children? Were they half-humans, half-beasts? You know dear Radhika, why so many rapes are committed all over the world? So many times, investigations of rapes reveal traces of skin found under the nails of the victims, denoting a struggle. We women have to train ourselves to decapitate and destroy their manhood forever. It only requires training to do that. In order to survive, we Israelis have to attack before we are attacked. No wonder Albert Einstein rightly said that the world will not be destroyed by those who do evil, but by those who watch them.'

'I realise how it has been for you all,' responded Radhika sympathetically. The pain, anguish and insecurity on the lovely face of Ziki was clearly visible. 'The Holocaust perpetuated on you people was by the civilized West. This is the saddest part. The animosity of the Arabs after the Second World War with regard to the creation of Israel came later.'

Ziki sighed, 'Ironically, of all religions, Christianity and Judaism are most similar. Both believe in the oneness of God, the eternal and infinite one, who is holy, righteous and just, while also loving, forgiving and merciful. Both share the same Hebrew scripture, the Old Testament. However, the Christians have the New Testament as well. Both believe that God has a special plan for the nation of Israel and the Jewish people.

'The critical difference is the person of Jesus Christ. Christians believe that Jesus is the fulfilment of old Testament prophesies of the coming of a Messiah and saviour. Judaism acknowledges Jesus to be a good teacher and even a prophet of God but does not believe him to be a Messiah. The religious leaders in Israel during Jesus' time are believed to have asked him, "Are you the Christ, son of the blessed one?" Jesus replied, "I am." But the leaders did not believe in his words.'

'But this much of a difference does not seem to be so much when seen in the context of the vast similarities and commonalities,' said Radhika. 'We, in Hinduism, have many such differences in our interpretations of our faith. This much of flexibility seems so natural when you interpret scriptures of such early times. What is the big deal? In any case, there are so many varied translations of all religious manuscripts. God is all about divinity, mercy, forgiveness, isn't it? For hundreds of centuries, human beings are trying to understand God and yet the quest is an ongoing process. So it shall be forever.' Ziki stared at Radhika. She appeared fascinated by Radhika's response. She was pensive for a while. Then, she took a long swig of the red wine and asked Radhika to talk a bit about the essence of Hindu religion.

Radhika said, 'Hinduism is the world's oldest living religion. It is richly diverse and spiritual in its essence. It is a set of core beliefs. Two of these core beliefs are oneness of existence and pluralism. It doesn't have one scripture alone as its anvil and is therefore flexible with no single founder. All beings, from the smallest of organisms to man are considered manifestations of the divine. So, the universe is a family and everyone is equal. No one is superior, none inferior. It believes that divinity manifests in different forms and can be worshipped by various means. 'It acknowledges the existence of more than one path to God.

Hinduism does not insist that one's own path to God is the only meaningful and true path. So Hinduism never sanctioned proselytizing. It has never invaded another land in the name of religion. Peaceful coexistence is its essence, thus in India eight major religions co-exist—Hinduism, Buddhism, Judaism, Christianity, Islam, Sikhism, Jainism and Zoroastrian. God is a matter of constant, never ending tradition of philosophical inquiry and debate. But the freedom given to us in interpreting our religion, have led to many fault lines being created like the caste system, introduction to plethora of rituals, domination of higher castes etc. So there is confusion as well.'

Ziki was listening very intently indeed. What amazed her was the fact that Radhika was discussing her religion without any restraint or hesitation, like a bird flying majestically in the open sky. 'So you have a plethora of prophets and sages. Being so old a religion, it must have spread in ancient times through word of mouth and hence with some distortions and confusions, I suppose,' queried Ziki.

'Oh yes. There have been plenty of prophets, sages, mythologies and surfeit of confusions. But the essence of the religion I just described remains,' replied Radhika laughing.

'Radhika let me know a bit about some prophets or sages in India who have influenced you the most.'

'There are quite a few. But I shall talk about the two who dominate my spiritual beliefs. One is Buddha. He insisted upon training oneself to attain final peace. He taught the concept of Eightfold path as follows:

- Right views, right intentions constitute wisdom.
- Right speech, right actions, right livelihood constitute morality.
- Right effort, right mindfulness and right concentration constitute concentration.

'Among founder of many religions, Buddha was a rare prophet or rather a teacher, who did not claim divine authority in any form. Buddhism today is more a philosophy than religion. It can be taught to others who are not Buddhists. In fact, Buddhism can be taught equally well by atheists. Dear Ziki, Indian spiritual thoughts have professed some useful wisdom through a set of simple questions.

- What is faster than the wind?—Mind
- What makes humans powerful?—Education
- What is more numerous than grass?—Thoughts
- What is the worst disease in humans?—Greed

- What is simplicity?—Equanimity
- What is man's most dreaded enemy?—Anger

'The Second spiritual leader was Guru Nanak. He stressed on the following:-

- There is only one God who is infinite who cannot die or be reincarnated, or assume human form.
- Renunciation of home, family, performance of rites and ceremonies, torment of body does not lead to enlightenment—only good deeds do.
- All human beings are equal and castes are created by man to retain superiority of the few.
- Charity, worship, hard work should be the ethical conduct of life.

'To create a casteless society, Nanak introduced the practice of free community kitchens for devotees of every caste and religion to eat together. He felt that greatest of all evils is ego. Once ego is conquered, other sins like anger, greed, lust, pride could be overcome. He also felt that poetry and devotional songs were important means of achieving wisdom and communion with God. This was in consonance with the Sufi devotion to Allah through this route. He shunned religious bigotry.'

Ziki was listening with such intensity to Radhika that she did not even remember to sip her wine till she had finished. Suddenly both of them noticed that a few others sitting around the bar were listening to their conversation with deep interest.

Later as Radhika and Ziki returned back to their hostel in Eilat, Ziki seemed keen to spend more time with her. Radhika was sleepy. She was accustomed to a glass of wine once in a while. Ziki pleaded for sharing a beer in her room. Radhika could not turn down the request. After all, in a few days time they would part forever. Radhika expressed her deep feeling of sympathy for both Israelis and the Palestinian civil population. She thought hard to coin a suitable term for them. She could only think of the term *Victims of Divinity*.

'Ziki, I am shocked to see the sufferings, pain and anguish as well as constant threat of insecurity, physical violence of the people of Israel and Palestine. This is the land where three major religions were born, the and of Prophets and Revelations from the divine all merciful God. It should be the most blessed place on earth. It actually is the most cursed and explosive region on earth. It all does not fit in. Something is fundamentally wrong. Why are human beings here, men, women, innocent children so insecure and forever suffering for thousands of years?'

'But violence and injustice are being perpetuated in the name of religion elsewhere too. Isn't it Radhika?' said Ziki.

'Yes of course that is true elsewhere also, all over the world. But dammit! this small little area comprising of Israel, Palestine and the surrounding land is the soil from which three religions arose. If the all merciful, all forgiving God carried out his revelations here, of all the other places on planet earth, he should have blessed this area. If ever there could have been a heaven on earth, it should have been here. This place should have been the centre of gravity of goodness, spirituality, mercy. The dilution of human values, spirituality and divinity should have taken place far, far away from this land,' said Radhika with great sincerity.

'Are you suggesting that religions have taken human beings for a ride?' asked Ziki.

'I don't know about that. Though human beings are always taking fellow humans for a ride if that helps them to gain power and all that which comes from power,' said Radhika.

Ziki spoke sadly, 'When Jews were being slaughtered en masse during Holocaust, the victims would have felt that there could not be a divine entity known as God. Otherwise he would have intervened. For all the slaughter was being done by

Christian nations against Jews, both of whom share the Bible, though with a bit of difference in interpretation about Jesus.'

Radhika remarked pensively, 'Ziki, ideology is the root cause of all violence. So, if religions do not preach harmony, peace, humanity and spiritual purity, they are not religions as they have nothing religious in their entity.' She further added, 'As per Indian philosophy, there are two types of victory in this world—Vijaya and Jaya. Vijaya is material victory where there are winners and losers. Jaya is spiritual victory where there are only victors, no losers.' Ziki replied, 'For Jews and Palestinians, there can neither be Jaya, nor Vijaya. We are under a curse to be forced to pitch our respective caravans on a small biblical oasis.'

Radhika concluded, 'Therefore, as per Hinduism, Buddhism, Sikhism in India, the search for God through multiple routes, thought processes must go on. It cannot be scripture bound and thus narrowed down to a laid down conclusion. The search has to be human, spiritual… an eternal search forever. It has to be an inward search.'

Ziki got up embraced Radhika. She was crying as well as smiling affectionately. These two were friends forever now.

'You Indians have something special in you. You are brought up differently Radhika. I have fallen in love with India even though I have never been there.'

'We also have lots of poverty, bad governance and petty politics. We have not yet done enough justice to our spiritual past and have a long way to go. And dear Ziki, you shall come to India one day. And mark my words, you Israelis have two advantages which I would call, in terms of Hinduism as Goddess Lakshmi and Saraswati.'

'What does that mean?'

'In Hinduism, Lakshmi is the Goddess of wealth and prosperity. You all, with your inherent capabilities, hard work, innovations, have ensured this. Saraswati is the goddess of learning and wisdom. You have a brain power which cannot be equalled anywhere. Through pursuance of that you have world class technology. Since in the ultimate analysis, the pen is mightier than the sword, you have both at your disposal. However, there is a danger which Israel must guard against. The combined power of pen and sword can cause arrogance. That is a toxic combo. You need to give a fair space for Palestinians to live with honour and dignity. That will not be easy because there is arrogance on the other side too. The solution for the rivalries existing here does not lie in scriptures, books, religion. It lies in the hearts and minds of all stakeholders. It is needless to say that this is the most difficult task.'

'Meanwhile,' replied a saddened Ziki, 'It is as if God has told all the Israelis, Palestinians, Muslims and Christian living here, "thou shall not seek an answer". Keep suffering. Perhaps, God is a cosmic delusion and we humans have been taken for a ride. I wonder if humans become atheists, but have character, values and compassion, the world will become more humane.'

She smiled to ease the serious discussion.

'Radhika, there is an old Jewish joke. It is about how if Moses had turned right instead of left when the proverbial Red Sea parted, the Israelis' would have ended up with the oil and Arabs with the oranges.' Radhika laughed, squeezing Ziki's hand.

'Ziki, I have read that recently numerous gas fields have been found in the Mediterranean Sea within the territorial waters of Israel. Production is expected to start in 2019. Massive explorations are on.'

'Yes, that is true. We should not only be self sufficient in our energy needs but also have a huge balance for export.'

'This has huge implications Ziki. It could open up a huge source of gas for Europe, reduce its dependency on Russia. It can transform relations between Israel and its neighbourhood. It can usher in peace.'

'Amen,' said Ziki.

The last trip Ziki and Radhika took together in Israel was to the Beersheba University. It was a beautiful drive from Jerusalem. How beautifully have the Israelis converted sections of the deserts into agriculturally productive green spaces. The cultivation by drip irrigation was done with such precision and efficiency, noted Radhika. Rich crops of fruits and vegetables were visible off and on, amidst sprawling mass of the desert. In the bus sat tourists of many nationalities. There was a smart boy with a pretty young girl. They were in their teens. They were wearing military uniforms and wielding a small weapon each. 'Those are Uzis. It is a combination of a rifle and a machine gun. They are deadly and agile weapons and these young kids are students in colleges. They do part time security duties. They earn some money which helps them pay their college fees. They are very well trained and can respond to situations in a flash,' explained Ziki.

'What about you Ziki?' asked Radhika.

'I too am trained, Radhika. In case of an emergency, during an attack if these two get killed or wounded, any Israeli in this bus is capable of dashing for these two Uzis to continue the fight. There would also be an odd person in this bus who is carrying a pistol somewhere on him or her.'

'My god Ziki, are things so bad?'

'No, not necessarily. The fact that we are always prepared and ready to fight back ensures that we are mostly safe. This is the gift to the people of this region from the three religions which were born here. They were born here so that we die here,' smiled Ziki.

Beersheba University was a huge sprawling place. Students from all over the world came here. The academic staff seemed extremely knowledgeable, focused and smart, as were the students. Ziki took Radhika all around the university. Both interacted with the faculty and students. Radhika was fascinated. Israel was a country that almost always was in a state of conflict for survival, not only as a nation but also as a race—yet, it had some of the best institutions of learning, research, technology, governance, policing, intelligence network globally, and was the finest military machine in the world. Here in this Biblical land, Israel was the embodiment of a veritable David, not at all afraid of the Goliaths all around.

They were to return to Jerusalem that evening. Ziki was determined to extend their stay in Beersheba by a day. She knew that soon Radhika would be flying back to India from Tel Aviv.

'There is no point in spending two days at Tel Aviv, Radhika. One day is enough before you leave for India. I am booking us at a nice hotel here,' pleaded Ziki, but very decisively. Radhika too thought it to be a good idea.

'Maybe we were twin sisters in one of our previous lives,' laughed Radhika.

'Where? In India or in Israel?' smiled Ziki.

'Who knows?' wondered Radhika.

'Why twins?'

'I don't know. It just flashed in my mind.'

The two spent the evening in Beesheba at a pub which was very classy and elegant. Two European men made a futile attempt to befriend them. 'One of them was definitely French,' laughed Ziki. 'Then the other one could well have been an Italian,' smiled Radhika.

Soon, over a pint of excellent beer, both started chatting.

'Tell me more about Indian philosophy and thoughts. Since you mentioned about previous life, we can start with that,' suggested Ziki.

Radhika said, 'Rebirth has always been a central teaching in Buddhism as well as Hinduism. Buddha searched for happiness wherein one need not be subjected to rebirth. In fact, he wanted to find freedom from rebirth and associated pains and tribulations of another life. The word Karma means volitional act. The law of Karma is the law of cause and effect. In simple terms it means every deed produces commensurate results. Karma means the effects created by intentional acts of body, speech and mind. Only acts devoid of desire, hate and delusion do not produce Karmic effects. Westerners often misinterpret it as fate or some kind of cosmic justice system. It is not so.'

Ziki asked, 'Can you explain this basic concept with a real life example?'

Radhika thought awhile and said, 'Someone goes to a bar, gets drunk, misbehaves with women and gets thrown out. He drives home angry, overruns a stray dog, injures a pedestrian en-route. He gets home, beats up his wife, scolds his protesting daughter. This is Karma in action. One angry act has generated many more disgusting Karmic acts. So, our past has some influence on our present. The present is also shaped by our actions here and now. What you do is what happens to you. To change our Karma we have to change our lives. There are no mysterious, cosmic forces out there. It is not about reward or punishment by a divine judge. There is no supreme God sitting in judgment over all of us.'

Ziki was now engrossed. She asked about rebirth. Radhika continued, 'Here there are two schools of thought. The classical Hindu understanding of reincarnation is that a soul is reborn many times. When the effects of karma continue across lifetimes, it causes rebirth. But the Buddhist understanding is that there is no soul or self. That which is reborn is not the same person yet not separate from the same person. Like every wave is a new wave, yet not different from the ocean. It is something like that. That is why, if we perceive God as the divine truth, the search has to be a continuous one, choosing different paths. Maybe we humans are not programmed to discover it. Instead of distorting it, it is better to continue the search as humble students do. Even the greatest thinkers and scientists have only managed to touch the tip of the iceberg in their spheres of speciality. So Ziki, Karma determines if there will be a reincarnation back into the world of *maya*.'

'What is *maya*?' queried Ziki.

'*Maya* is all that is not divine. *Maya* is the veil that hides the Absolute, the supreme. *Maya* is God's act of self concealment. Yoga is the disciplined effort to experience the Absolute, the Divine. Therefore, Buddha suggests that a person's good or bad actions, karma, result in better or worse reincarnations. The highest goal consists of release, called Nirvana from this cycle of rebirths. Our *Bhagavad Gita* says that true devotion to any deity or belief system will lead those devotees who have compassion and mercy to God.'

'Hmm!' exclaimed Ziki. 'Interesting. I suppose, if only we humans stopped this farce of knowing God and concentrate on being better human beings, life would be better.'

'Yes indeed,' pondered Radhika. 'This is the biggest "if only" of human existence. Ultimately, we humans need to rise to the highest pedestal of being—is the level where we humans learn to be good without expecting anything.'

Radhika looked out of the window of the aircraft as it took off from Tel Aviv airport. She felt a wave of emotions as she looked down upon the Israeli soil with the rhythmic waves of the Mediterranean softly touching its coastline as if caressing it with love and assurance. The coast was full of Israelis and tourists, lying, sitting along the shore, children splashing around, all trying to live a normal life amidst the ever present threat of violence and potential conflict situations just forty odd miles to its East, North, South. She had been so right in deciding to go on a foreign trip and be on her own for a few weeks. Radhika, the young lady had transformed herself into a woman of substance, a different human being indeed. No American diamond would impress her any longer. Only a solitaire guy could share her life with her hereafter, and that would be a problematic scenario. But then, where is the hurry? she thought, as her mother's face came to her mind.

Arvind in Malaysia

> No man is an island entire of itself; every man
> is a piece of the continent, a part of the main;
> —John Donne.

Arvind was happy to get a good job with Glaxo Smith Kline (GSK). His place of posting was Kuala Lumpur, Malaysia. Initially, after his two years stay in Singapore while doing MBA, he was a bit sceptical about Malaysia. As an Indian, he was in for a surprise. On reaching Kuala Lumpur, he found Malaysia to be so much more advanced than India that it embarrassed him. It looked to him as if Malaysia was knocking at the doors to be recognised as a developed country. He found India to be at least two decades behind Malaysia in so many parameters. The infrastructure in Malaysia was superior in terms of quality of roads, highways, drainage, hygiene and sanitation, quality of town and country planning and greenery. The size, magnitude and imaginative designs of houses, condos, malls, shopping centres, parking facilities, parks, sports facilities, toilets and other services were qualitatively at par with the developed world.

The civilized behaviour of the people towards each other,

propensity to observe existing rules, regulations, the sense of propriety, tolerance to diverse cultural tapestry, including foreign tourists were remarkably visible. Women could safely drive back home late at night. There was scope for healthy activities in all tourist spots. Tourism was well organised, with high quality of infrastructure and facilities, imaginatively planned and laid out. The police were smart, looked well trained, efficient, well in control. Everyone driving on the excellent roads and highways was abiding by the rules. One could hardly see chaotic reckless driving, uncivilized overtaking and horn blowing. Not a single two wheeler was ridden without helmets. Observing rules and regulations seemed so natural to the citizens.

Oh my God! What have we done to ourselves in India in the last seven decades? gasped Arvind. He hardly saw any beggars. Beggars are seen in such large numbers around the streets of cities like Delhi, Kolkata, Mumbai and also in smaller towns and cities. They are also there in large numbers outside temples, railway platforms, begging for money or food. They look so dirty, malnourished, with children along with them. They are in trains, bus stops, outside eating places, living on street pavements, under flyovers, bridges. Hundreds are frozen to death during winters, sleeping on pavements. Arvind remembered Ayan telling him that in India, the poor beg outside and the rich, many of whom are the most corrupt, beg inside the temples.

Arvind noted an article on rise in obesity amongst police in Malaysia. Concerns were raised about the fact that ten per cent of the police force was overweight. People doubted the ability of obese policemen to control crime whenever it took place. In India, almost fifty per cent of police force appeared obese everywhere. Yet, this was hardly a matter of national concern. The article in the newspaper went on to explain how overweight policemen and officers were being officially warned to shape up fast, before their promotions and pay increments got blocked, threatening premature retirement after a specified time. It was also suggested that a ministerial body be created which would monitor all aspects of regular training and retraining of the police in Malaysia to prepare them to handle complex internal security situations as and when they arose.

Arvind, during weekends and holidays, visited various tourist spots in Malaysia. Similar to the developed world, a vast majority of Malaysians leave home during weekends along with family and children, towards a plethora of tourist spots. Arvind visited Langkawi, Malacca, a beautifully laid out hill station of Cameron Highlands, hot springs, Genting Heights, French Village, Rainforests etc. In all these exotic places, he observed tourists from all over the developed world enjoying the well laid out tourist facilities, without any worry or fear. Whether it was the taxi drivers, conductors of excellent and spotlessly clean buses, hotel managers, room service staff in hotels, guides, policemen, shop keepers—all were impeccable in their behaviour and dealings. Even if on many occasions language was a problem, one did not feel bad. Both sides tried to make the other understand till someone helped them out.

He was also struck by the Indian origin people, mostly Tamils. They were quite prosperous. Many of them were extraordinary success stories. On a Sunday, Arvind was taken to a Gujarati eating place in a locality called Taman Bukit Pantai, Bangsar. The name of the place was *The Ganga Cafe*. It was run by a Gujarati lady who originally was from Mumbai though she used the word Bombay. It was mid-day. The capacity of *Ganga Café* was about two hundred. It was jam-packed, with scores of people waiting for tables to be cleared. Arvind saw an amazing sight. Seventy per cent of customers were Malays, Chinese Malays and Western tourists. All the Malaysians and foreign tourists were avid non-vegetarians. Yet they were there in *Ganga Café* which only offered Gujarati vegetarian food of all varieties. *Dal*, many types of vegetable preparations, *pakoras*, *khakhras*, assortment of pickles, varieties of *rotis*, rice, *ghee*, were being consumed with great relish. It looked as if the taste buds of Malaysians had undergone a major transformation.

Arvind noticed a large Chinese family with many children. A young girl of about five years was being encouraged to eat the *masala* food. As she put food in her mouth, she would cry out due to the chilli content, but the parents, encouraged her to eat on.

The elderly lady who ran this café was one of the many success stories of Indian origin Malaysians. Similarly, in Langkawi, Arvind saw some more such success stories. Cameroon Highlands is a beautiful, lush, green hill station, about four hours drive from Kuala Lumpur.

There was a sprawling strawberry farm spread along the slope of a hill. The sight of abundant juicy strawberries growing on terraced slopes, extending for few kilometres was beautiful. Along with this fruit, there were areas growing choicest varieties of vegetables, flowers, orchids, herbs. As one climbed the central steps up the slope, there were places where one could rest and admire the surroundings. If ever one could imagine the Garden of Eden, this could be the one. As you went on, there were places where you could buy things grown there. Adequate facilities of spotlessly clean, hygienic toilets, food stalls were available. Parents and grandparents were seen moving along with small children ensuring that they did not extend their hands through the nets covering the produce, to pluck anything. Obeying rules, regulations and not indulging in improprieties seemed so much a part of their upbringing and conduct.

Arvind savoured this experience. He felt proud when on a huge display board he read that this productive enterprise was started many decades ago by a Tamil couple settled in Malaysia for generations. It was started in an embryonic fashion on a small piece of land just to earn a living. The couple gradually increased the area in small instalments since local people started buying the produce. Since the hill slope was cheap to acquire, it kept growing. The local government authorities were impressed and facilitated this productive enterprise. They were also happy with the fact that some local Malays were employed by the Tamil couple. It soon grew to become a win-win situation and tourists started visiting this complex on their way down from Cameroon Highlands. They bought the fresh strawberries, jams, toppings, fresh exotic vegetables and plants etc. Thus was created a veritable Garden of Eden.

Today, lakhs of tourists visit this venture, enjoy a couple of hours here, eat and drink in the small, imaginative food court which offers healthy snacks and meals. Some hotels and dormitories have mushroomed at this spot wherein tourists can halt for a couple of days, hiking around in the sylvan surroundings.

This Tamil couple is an exemplary case of success and capability of the Indian origin diaspora not only in Malaysia but many other places in South East Asia and the rest of the world.

Similar was the experience in Langkawi, a beautiful island with ninety small, lovely, lush green islands dotting the seas all around it. There is a beautiful Tea Garden resort where thousands of tourists visit. Sipping a wide array of flavoured tea, grown in the tea plantations all around, one marvels at the lush green surroundings, hills and streams. This complex too is the creation of an Indian origin Malaysian.

Arvind was so happy to see the power of Indian creativity, culture, spreading slowly and steadily in Asia. Even some Indian commercial films, with their elaborate settings, music, songs, very rhythmic, graceful classical based dances were being viewed by South East Asians with increasing popularity. Meaningful films like *Piku, Taare Zamee Par, Three Idiots, PK* and even *Bajrangi Bhaijan* were popular in South East Asia and China.

However, when some of these people visit India as tourists, what all they experience amidst the din, bustle, dust and chaos of India is a different matter. In India you can travel hundreds of miles on its poor quality roads without finding clean toilets for ladies or other basic facilities of international standards. From being a typical rich Delhite living in his own ivory tower, Arvind was now growing into a global citizen with a broad vision, ready to call a spade a spade and face up to the bottom line in India, yet not losing hope. No wonder, Mr Narendra Modi, realising the potential of soft power of India spreading all over the globe by creative, productive and peaceful Indian Diasporas is encouraging them to scale greater heights abroad. Buddhism and Indian Diaspora are two entities which have grown and prospered on leaving Indian shores. India has to reap this Asian Dividend in this Asian Century. It has to start doing it very soon, otherwise decades of this century will roll on anyway, leaving it gasping and lagging behind.

Meanwhile, Arvind watched with great interest and pride the Prime Minister of India on TV addressing young start-up entrepreneurs. He was so happy to note that India ranked third globally behind USA and UK in start-ups and ambitious plans were being made to help such enterprising young people.

Working with GSK was a great experience. The small team of seven in which Arvind worked comprised of two Malaysians, one Chinese, a Singaporean and an Australian, apart from the boss who was from UK. John Brown was an efficient, hardworking, yet friendly boss. He trusted his team mates. At least, once every month, on the first Monday, he would take his team out for drinks and snacks or a dinner. One day Arvind asked him, 'John, why do you take us all out only on Mondays?'

John answered, 'Monday is the screwiest day for human beings. If every working morning in office seems like a Monday to people, then it becomes necessary to revaluate the status of the job. So, if we can make Mondays more bearable, the week can be more productive. I would like my team to get out of the Monday blues. We must share some jokes, take an extra half an hour break to liven up each other and brighten up the Mondays. So, if you guys see my unhappy face on a Monday, never think I am unhappy with you. I can assure you that if and when I shall become unhappy about your performances, I shall first introspect about my own. Thereafter, I shall let you all know about my concerns. So, there is no need for you to speculate. Work hard and let us sail together.'

This is the way a boss treats his subordinates in other parts of the world, outside India, pondered Arvind. In such an environment, the subordinates would always put in their best effort in their jobs. How could one let down one's boss by doing otherwise? If a team does not perform well, the heads of the organisation would sack the boss or the non performing members. It is as simple as that. In foreign firms, they choose and groom their subordinates to become leaders who can manage and not managers who cannot lead. Working under such a good manager, the subordinates cannot help giving their best.

During one such chat John initiated a discussion on the prospects and implications of the anticipated rise of Asia in this twenty-first century. He suggested that each one of his team first talk for a few minutes about their frank opinion regarding their own country in the context of the rise of Asia.

John asked Arvind to start the informal proceedings. Arvind started hesitatingly wondering why John had nominated him as the first speaker.

'Before Independence, our struggle in India was dominated by political rights, rather than our social duties. As a race we Indians must have been aware of our social duties. With centuries of subordination that consciousness may have died. After nearly seventy years of Independence, we are still rights conscious and not enough duty conscious. So to participate meaningfully in the rise of Asia, India needs a mass movement to inculcate duty consciousness and an intellectual renaissance. Presently I feel India is in a grip of an unhealthy melancholy. It is the cumulative effect of seven decades of poor performance, not commensurate with its vast potential.

'Asia is on the cusp of incredible opportunities. India needs to leverage technology, augment individual talent which it possesses, start-ups, collective capabilities, far better delivery of governance and increase its comprehensive national capabilities. Indian bureaucrats are suited, booted but not really rooted. Some of them are pretty ossified, rigid, arrogant—antithesis of dynamism. It they do not break barriers of their own making and rise to the occasion, India maybe a laggard elephant of Asia… huge but too slow.

'I feel our challenges are vast, deep and complex. India now is fully engaged with them. It is nudging itself forward. The rest of Asia knows that India's rise is essential to Asia's rise. Similar problems exist in all nations of Asia. So rise of Asia has to be a collective enterprise.'

John smiled appreciatively. 'So Arvind, what do you think India needs most today?'

'Well, it is difficult to answer this question in a concise form,' said Arvind. 'It certainly needs a moral compass as far as governance and political leadership are concerned. It needs a fresh dose of patriotism, the effect of which must linger on for a few decades, so as to get embedded into the national DNA. The last thing India needs is an irrational and delusional exuberance.

'Perhaps, there should be less of argumentativeness and more of intellectualism and productivity. We need to self reflect, introspect and wherever necessary, we need to shame ourselves for the state of the nation. We also need to realise that national interest in its widest sense is equal to patriotism. Presently the obsession for people in India is—which political party will come to power after five years? It is also affected by crude patriotism or political patriotism which is patriotism as defined by political class.'

There was a few seconds of silence. John said, 'Spoken from the heart, Arvind. We kind of feel your deep love for your nation which made you pull no punches.'

Arvind smiled and said, 'John, I think I am representative of the fourth and upcoming fifth generation of Indians since independence. They feel what I have expressed. We are aware of our potential and we are global in our perspectives. We feel we deserve far better leadership at the political level than we are being subjected to. We want to grow together with our fellow Asians as well as with the Western world, in a healthy, competitive environment for mutual benefit.'

Chang smiled. 'Arvind, answer this in one sentence only. Where lies the greatest strength of India?'

Arvind reflected for a while.

'It lies in India's pluralism, social, cultural and religious diversity and its ability to blend it all with the idea of India.'

Chang looked impressed. 'And where lies the greatest weakness of India?'

Arvind reflected on this question for a while longer.

'Ironically in these very factors I mentioned, if it does not manage these diversities well.'

Chang thought and then spoke. 'Therefore, I suppose any depreciation of diversity and eulogisation of uniformity will be the greatest challenge during the twenty-first century.'

The whole team nodded in agreement.

'So, in the words of John F Kennedy,

"The time to repair the roof is when the sun is shining."

'So let us all repair the Asian roof as it rises during this century,' concluded Arvind.

There was a deep sense of satisfaction on the face of John. It seemed that his aim of team building was being achieved during this session. GSK would not mind such small expenditures, which would give bigger dividends to this giant company in terms of performances by its able employees, selected so carefully.

John looked at Chang and said, 'Let us hear a few words on China in the context of Asian sunrise.'

Chang smiled and said, 'With typical Chinese restraint, I will be concise. You all have to provoke or push me a bit to make me more talkative. We, the fourth and fifth generation of Chinese have no fondness for politics. We are, however, very much involved with China's financial growth which must continue. This process started in 1979. India kick-started its economic liberalization in 1991, within the framework of its democratic system. China increased its momentum and leapfrogged ahead very fast. While democracy allows people to change the political masters, we do not feel the need to do so as long as the economy grows.

'Democracy is perhaps most suitable in developed societies where all people are well educated and can exercise their choices wisely. But elsewhere, in underdeveloped, poor yet democratic regions, people may soon realise that there are no political parties which inspire the nation. Then there arises a problem. This can delay progress. In the same context, a nation like China has grown in stature for over last four decades substantially and redeemed its glory. So we Chinese do not feel that such massive progress could have happened without great political leadership. Like all countries, we too have problems. But in every decade we do correct some of our fault lines and the fruits of progress are felt by the people.

'Therefore, in the future rise of Asia, we need not worry too much about our different systems of governance. It is for the people of the respective countries to decide what they want. The countries of Asia can definitely rise collectively respecting each other's systems. We can learn from each other. We can be different, yet develop a common goal for progress. This should be the new theme of the twenty-first century. China and India need to be wired together for this change and our generation must start this process now. For China and its people the opiate is massive progress and development. Creation of hundreds of millions of jobs within a reasonable time frame must be achieved. For us, patriotism lies in delivery of good governance, economic growth and diligent work ethos, never doing anything which will harm China, with disciplined and good behaviour.'

John looked at Arvind and asked him for his response. Arvind smiled and said, 'I agree with Chang completely. Democracy can fail the people just as communism also can, though the Chinese government has not yet failed its people. Rather, it has raised China's stature globally. So Chang and his generation who are beneficiaries of this enormous growth cannot complain. In India, democracy is degenerating despite the voting power of 100 per cent of people. The first 20 per cent hardly vote. Our generation of Indians have to suffer abysmal governance where we see the comprehensive loot of the nation in front of us.'

John interjected, 'But isn't corruption a big problem in China too Chang?'

'Yes it is,' answered Chang without hesitation. 'But we too see severe punishment being meted out to the most powerful people, often. Moreover, our huge economic growth acts as a balm for this, as restoration of our national stature. Global recognition of our performance does make up for such issues that we too face. That makes a huge difference.'

'Or can it be assumed that those at the helm of affairs in China, despite some failures on their part are more focused on China's national interests than other nations of Asia?' prodded John.

Chang did not respond.

Kuan from Singapore said, 'That is true.'

Chang smiled and nodded. 'We Chinese do not yet play cricket. But we prefer that the bat and the ball do the talking.' Everyone smiled at this truism.

John said, 'Finally Chang, what about the role of religion in China?'

Chang said thoughtfully, 'The Chinese system is presently engrossed as it should be towards maximising economic progress and restoring Chinese pride and self esteem. While doing so, it will, at an appropriate time, stretch itself to absorb, accommodate religious aspirations of the Chinese people, with conditions applied. National interest by itself is a state religion in China, in a manner of speaking. Other aspects of religions or religious beliefs will be officially kept in the private domain, as long as they too promote the national interest of China.'

'So what about Singapore in context of Asian century, Kuan?'

'We are a minuscule micro nation in Asia only in terms of size and population. However, in terms of a developmental model, administrative capabilities, organised, disciplined society, progressive dispensation, coexistence albeit within strictly laid down laws and rules, we have a macro role in Asia. We are striving to continue as the Jewel in the crown of Asia. The peaceful rise of Asia is critical to Singapore and the model of Singapore is critical to the Asian century.'

'Well said Kuan,' said Arvind and Chang together. Finally John looked at Abdul. 'We all are living and working so comfortably in Malaysia, what do you have to say?'

'Well, some of the good things of Singapore have also

motivated Malaysia. This is an Islamic nation which believes in secular coexistence and wants to be always in progressive mode. Although present glut of oil in the world and crash of oil prices have temporarily affected our economic growth, we all are trying to deal with this reality. We have huge oil resources. But we also have in us discipline, hunger for development and increasingly skilled manpower. We are also very tolerant. Our human resource is a mix of Malays, Chinese origin citizens, Indians, others. We too have our problems. Malaysia will remain a useful partner in the gigantic process of Asian century.'

Ayan's Ethereal Bonding

One fine sunny winter morning in Prague, Johnson decided to send Ayan to London for a four week assignment. 'Ayan, you will be part of an important project in London. You shall get the experience of working with a diverse group of people there. It will add value to your skill and job experience. Towards the end of the project, you shall be attending an international seminar where you shall represent our company. The subject of this seminar will be "Rise of Asia—Phoenix or Bubble?" Ayan was excited. He was very focused on subjecting himself to widest exposure during the first five years of his job. After that he would re-evaluate how to shape his life's priorities. So he was grateful for this exposure that his boss had planned for him. He wanted to broaden his intellectual horizon as much as possible.

Ayan spoke to Sneha at Cambridge University. 'Hi Sneha, how are you doing in the pristine, intellectual environment of Cambridge. You must have already mastered your research within six months of your work.'

'Hi Ayan, stop overestimating me so much. I am at sea *yaar.* There is so much more to learn. I am quite dissatisfied with my performance so far. My guide, Mary Chick, is such an intellectual, thinks so deep. Any session with her on my work opens up new arenas of my subject. Ayan, you are sounding very upbeat and excited.'

'Yes Sneha, I am. I am coming to London for a little over four weeks next month for a project. I shall be put up somewhere close to London Bridge.'

'Ayan, this is excellent news indeed. There is so much to talk about. I am so happy.'

'Yes indeed, Sneha. How is your brother Govind doing in the Army?'

'Govind is doing fine and proud to be soldiering. Presently he is near Jaisalmer, in Rajasthan, for training. He will be going for a junior officer's course to Deolali, near Nagpur, after a few months.'

'Great,' exclaimed Ayan. 'I will mail you the details of my trip to UK. Take care and don't become too serious and stern while studying in Cambridge. Your subject of research is a very serious one but it should not turn you into a different "you". You are good as you are. I am confident that a very meaningful life awaits you. Don't forget to put the music on as you study. Eat lots of fruits and vegetables. They are very delicious out there I am told, and Sneha, take life a bit more casually.'

'Yah, Yah. I spoke to Radhika. She has returned from a great trip abroad and has sent me a detailed mail on her experiences. See you soon Ayan. I have to rush to my college for an interaction. Take care bye. And by the way, you have lots of talent, communication skills, honesty, with practically no ego or idiosyncrasies. But take life a little more seriously as the world is a complex one.'

As Sneha disconnected her phone, she pondered, How

similar is Ayan to my brother Govind? Always acting like a protective guardian angel.

ଔ

Ayan landed at Heathrow Airport. There was quite a rush at the immigration as flights from India—Jet Airways and Air India had landed simultaneously. As he moved slowly in the long queue, he observed interesting facets of how people from different nations behave on arrival in Europe. The most disciplined were the Chinese tourists, standing patiently in line, including their children. They were intently observing the awkward behaviour of so many arrivals without any expression on their faces, even when someone pushed their handbags or brushed against their bodies in a hurried attempt to inch forward. Indian, Pakistani and Bangladeshi arrivals were their usual talkative selves, complaining about the wait. Many of them made no effort to control their children from disturbing others.

The security officers were busy keeping an eye on everyone in the huge crowd of arrivals. Whenever they noticed an old lady looking tired, or a mother with a few children looking harassed, they would escort them ahead of the queue so as to fast track them. Occasionally, they would also smile indulgently at the arrivals and tell them to keep their documents ready and that it would not take very long to clear the immigration. A child of a harassed looking mother was crying non-stop. A smiling official walked up to the child, took out a chocolate from his pocket and offered it. The child took it and stopped crying. When an odd guy tried to break the queue by cutting through the taped line, the official was annoyed. He firmly asked the violator to go back to his place. 'Not done,' he would say loudly. An Indian couple watching this felt ashamed. They spoke to the violators jumping the line in Hindi, '*Meharbani karke, aise harkat naa karen. Kyon hamare mulk ko badnam karte hain*?' (Please do not do this. Why do you bring a bad name to our country?)

Ayan pondered as he observed all this. Why do we do this and disgrace ourselves. What is it in us that prevents us from observing expected behaviour patterns and complying with rules and procedures. Even if a few of our people behave this way, they stand out amidst other foreigners.

As Ayan sat in a taxi, Arif, the smartly attired driver asked, 'Sir, which part of India do you live in?' Ayan replied that he was from Indore in Central India.

'My ancestors used to live in a village in Punjab before partition, Sir. They owned a lot of land there and grew very good quality rice.'

'How long have you lived here in UK now?' asked Ayan.

'I was born here. I am a third generation Pakistani.'

'So, as a third generation British citizen, how much do you miss Pakistan?'

'We go there off and on, certainly once every two years to our ancestral town in our side of Punjab. Our roots are there after all.'

'You get all the rights and privileges on offer as the citizens of UK. That must be very convenient.'

'Yes Sir. Here all citizens are entitled to free medical and free education and even government housing for those who are poor and unemployed. But there are other problems too.'

'What type of problems?' queried Ayan.

'Sir, they are largely cultural and social problems. There are many things done here which are against our culture and religion. Women here are too modern and fast. That influences our women. The women here dress so boldly, drink, hug and kiss on the streets, in the trains etc. Our children can get spoilt here, you see.'

'But Arif, you are the third generation in your family since you migrated here. Do you feel you have been spoilt by living amidst the Britishers? I am sure you have blended well and yet your roots are intact; perhaps have actually improved by picking up the good aspects of the British people. In this world we need to learn so much from each other, isn't it?'

'Yes, I suppose. But my children may not be as guarded as we were against wrong influences,' replied Arif.

'In that case Arif, we are all free to go back to our roots. And how do we assure ourselves about the nature of our roots which have taken form in our respective countries? How safe will our children be there? If our respective countries are better than UK or Europe, then of course one must return, isn't it?'

Arif was quiet. He was absorbing the inputs from Ayan. After a while, Ayan resumed the discussion. 'My friend, I can only share with you what I feel on this subject. I may be wrong. If I decide to settle down in the developed Western world, firstly I will apply for it. Once permission is granted, I shall be grateful for it and perhaps throw a party in India for my friends and relatives to celebrate my good luck. Then I shall have to adapt myself and integrate with the culture and traditions of the citizens here while holding on to my own origins as well. No one is going to force me to change my faith certainly not in this part of the world. If there were better prospects in my own country why should I have come here? So for us, this place is better than our own in the overall sense.'

'But sir, we have to protect our private lives, our religious beliefs. What is wrong with that?' asked Arif.

'This is a very interesting question, Arif. Our lives are partly in the private space and partly in the public space. You are no exception. The constitution, judicial system in developed countries tries to protect a virtually unlimited sphere of private beliefs as no other part of the world does. But if I am a waiter here, I cannot demand that I will not serve women who are boldly dressed as per our thinking. As a life guard, will I not go to save a woman wearing a bikini from drowning? If my private beliefs are so overwhelmingly important to me then I should never leave my home to go abroad to seek a better life. Isn't this a fair way of looking at things? Think about it please.'

Arif just nodded his head thoughtfully. Ayan appreciated the fact that Arif was impressionable to good logic. So he thought of continuing the discussion a bit more.

'Moreover Arif, in this second decade of our twenty-first century, we have to coexist as a human race. We can have different faiths, just as we have different food habits, clothes, cultures, colours. It is up to us to ensure that we groom and bring up our children as good human beings who can work, earn, and live together. Is this car yours or are you only driving it?'

'This is my own car. We are three brothers. One brother is running a family owned corner shop, another owns a meat shop. I have a fleet of three cars that ply as taxis. The other two cars are run by fellow Pakistanis. We have our own small flats and our children go to state schools in our borough near Croydon. Sir, *Inshallah*, we live quite well.'

'That is very good Arif. Well done. Your children will do even better since I am aware that government run schools in UK are very well funded with good facilities. Hope you take my discussion in the right spirit. After all, we Indians and Pakistanis are like cousins in an erstwhile joint family, isn't it?'

Arif smiled. 'That is so true, sir. I am glad to have met you. However, we do worry about our daughters coming under the influence of Western culture.'

'What about the sons, Arif?'

Arif just smiled and said, 'We have reached central London sir. Your destination is only ten minutes or so away.'

On reaching his hotel Ayan happily gave ten pounds extra.

'Take it Arif, after all we are erstwhile cousins. Get a cake for your children. Have a good weekend.'

Ayan settled down in the hotel. It was a decent place providing all amenities and comforts, with breakfast included. He rang up Sneha. A very happy Sneha asked him to meet her at the Tower Hotel near the London Bridge next day at 11 am. 'Tower Hotel is just a mile from your hotel. Walk it and enjoy the journey. We shall be there. Welcome to England, Ayan, I can't wait to meet you.'

'Who is the "we" part, Sneha?' asked Ayan smiling.

'That is a surprise,' laughed Sneha.

'Oh, are you seeing some guy *yaar*. I am glad. Hope he is intelligent and serious,' said Ayan.

'Shut up and see you tomorrow.'

Ayan enjoyed the walk from his hotel *Holiday Inn Express*. It took him about twenty minutes to reach the general area of London Bridge. It had the Tower Bridge on one side and the Millennium Bridge on the other—all three bridges spanning the Thames River. He noticed the imposing wall of the Tower of London.

Being a Saturday, the entire area had a festive look. Ayan noticed a van selling ice creams. The seller was a young boy helping his dad, perhaps. He was wearing a red plastic cover on his nose. He was looking like a joker. As children crowded around for ice-cream, he was entertaining them with funny gestures. The children giggled, with their indulgent parents smilingly watching. The way ice creams of all varieties were being sold, the mobile shop would be running out of stock soon. A very smart young Chinese couple passed by pushing a colourful pram. Inside were two beautiful kids. They appeared to be twins. So many people walking around admired the kids. Some said, 'God bless them.' The proud Chinese couple smilingly moved on.

As Ayan strolled along, he noticed an old man playing a

guitar with full concentration. He appeared to be poor. He was playing rather well. His selection of songs was very good. Some tunes were from *My Fair Lady*, *Sound of Music* and others of old vintage. Tourists would stop near him and enjoy the music; some would place coins on a small sheet of cloth spread on the ground in front of him. What impressed Ayan was the poise of the poor old man. He was totally engrossed in his guitar. He didn't even look at the alms being given. He couldn't be playing the guitar so well unless he was formally trained. Wonder what must be the story of his life? Technically, he was not begging. He was entertaining people with his skill and leaving it to them to decide whether to pay him or not. There was dignity in his poverty. He was fighting it bravely. Ayan put down a five pound note. The old man would never know who gave such a handsome amount. He was not even looking towards it.

As Ayan walked on, he noticed an elderly British couple. The old man was in a wheelchair. The old lady was limping along slowly. They would occasionally stop for a while and chat with each other. They had to speak loudly to each other to be heard. They looked so much in love, together trying to deal with their age and physical condition. They must be staying in some old age home nearby. They looked rich enough. They also looked very determined.

Ayan reached the Tower Hotel almost exactly at 11 am. The place overlooked the Thames with the towering and magnificent London Bridge to the left. Chairs and tables were neatly laid outdoors and all were occupied by the cheerful weekenders, all having fun. Some elderly people, seemingly grandparents of some of the children playing around, and casually dressed couples were amusing themselves, watching the children run around them. An elderly couple were sitting quietly. The gentleman was reading a newspaper while the old lady was gazing at the Thames River. Two half filled jugs of beer were waiting to be sipped.

Ayan was overjoyed to identify Sneha amongst the crowd. As Sneha saw Ayan, she came bounding towards him. They hugged and shook hands. Sneha took a good look at Ayan. 'You are looking smart. You are looking less kiddish than you were in Singapore.' Holding his hand, she took him towards a table under a colourful umbrella. Ayan saw a very pretty young lady sitting there. She looked as if not only her immaculate dress but she herself had just come out of the laundry. He found it difficult to avoid looking at her more than it was proper.

'Meet Li Na, my friend. Li, this is my best friend Ayan, I was talking to you about. They shook hands and settled down. Both the ladies were having a gin and tonic. Sneha said, 'I am sure you will have some beer as usual Ayan.'

'Yes please. Hereafter I am taking over as far as drinks and lunch are concerned. Among us, I am the one who has a job. Sneha, you are still a student and therefore my junior. I suppose Li is too,' smiled Ayan. He hoped that his smile still had the same charm his friends had certified in Singapore.

Sneha said, 'Ayan, Li is doing her Masters in English Language from Cambridge. She is about to finish the course. She is from Singapore.'

'That is interesting indeed,' said Ayan,

The next two hours passed so fast. Sneha spoke about how her research was progressing. Ayan spoke about his experiences in Prague. Li Na spoke about her studies and experiences in the United Kingdom. Li Na was a natural conversationalist, though she chose her words very professionally and aptly. Ayan noticed that what Li Na could express in two sentences, Indians like him and Sneha would do in ten. She was a Singaporean of Chinese origin. Her family had been living in Singapore and she had never been to India.

After asking for their preferences for lunch, Ayan ordered three plates of fish and chips, adding salad with garlic bread.

The threesome ate the food with great gusto and the plates were bereft of a single morsel of food. Later, they explored the London Tower nearby.

'Do not worry too much about the gory past history of London Tower. Just enjoy its architecture and the present ambience inside. Also know that lakhs of beautiful plastic poppies were pinned outside the tower, one each for every British soldier who died during the World War. The whole nation of England honours and remembers them with deep respect, pride and emotion,' explained Sneha.

'So nice,' said Ayan. 'Great are the nations who honour and remember their soldiers. India is quite far from that stage yet. My parents watched the last London Olympics and noted that a part of the various stadiums were reserved for the British military persons.'

Sneha noted a strange blend of sadness and anger on the face of Ayan. He would always remain emotional on this issue, being the son of an army officer, she thought looking at Ayan affectionately.

'Okay Ayan. Next time we meet, it will be in Trafalgar Square. And you have to spend a weekend in Cambridge too. There are some decent places to stay in there,' said Sneha, holding Ayan's hand once again.

'Nice to have met you Ayan,' said Li Na with a smile that was mesmerising, yet purely natural. 'See you again.'

While returning in a bus to Cambridge, Li Na looked at Sneha and said smilingly, 'You two are very fond of each other. Ayan is a nice guy. So natural, unpretentious, intelligent, with an air of sensitivity and character around him. Any girl would feel totally safe and comfortable with him.'

'You are so right in your analysis about a guy you just met for the first time. Your observation amazes me. You are a good judge of human beings. It is a great asset you have,' replied Sneha.

After a pause while staring out of the window at the beautiful picture postcard landscape, Sneha continued, 'Yes, I was always fond of him but in a different way. When I left home and family for the first time to go to Singapore, I was missing the protective presence of my brother. Meeting Ayan instantly reminded me of my brother. His looks, the way he talks, jokes, his mannerisms are quite like my brother.'

'I felt that you both were very comfortable with each other,' prodded Li Na. 'Come on Sneha, tell me.'

'You are wrong there Li Na. I am older to him. He looks a few years younger than his age. He is a very well brought up, upright guy. He deserves a different type of a girl from a serious, contemplative, over analysing girl like me. He would not be able handle a girl like me. I like him a lot and respect him too. He also is very fond of his military roots as he has spent his childhood in military cantonments in India with his parents. I would always wish him the best in his life. Hope a good, cheerful girl grabs him in due course of time. She would be very lucky indeed.'

Ayan had to work quite hard during the project. It was a very satisfying experience. He learnt quite a lot from his colleagues, from each one of them. The guys from the West would work intently, looking serious, focused during work. During a coffee break, they would switch off their work demeanour completely and chat, laugh, enjoying their drink and then switch back to their serious stance, when back at work. The Japanese and the Chinese guys would remain pretty serious during work as well as during breaks. Even with a mug of coffee or juice they would be still immersed mentally in their assignments. Probably they were culturally adapted to the quest for constant and never ending improvement of their output. They were nice, friendly, correct in their behaviour, though. Probably they would prefer to have the drink and continue working without having to get out of their work stations.

Ayan preferred the Western model of work culture which was efficient, output oriented, yet a bit more laid back. He also appreciated the Western penchant for a five day week. For them, weekend was personal space, quite inviolable except on occasions demanding a serious need to violate it. Then they would cheerfully rise to the occasion. For them working late in the office as a habit was neither good for them nor for their families and definitely did not auger well for the organisation. It was not a positive reflection on the efficiency of the team or group. In the Western concept, social and personal interaction between employees improves communication skills, enhances interpersonal skills and quality, as well as balance in life and work. So much to learn, imbibe, mused Ayan to himself.

At the end of a busy, yet enjoyable four week project, Ayan felt he had evolved professionally equivalent to at least six months of work experience. Meanwhile, he could spend an excellent Sunday each with Sneha and Li Na, once at Trafalgar Square and another in Cambridge.

> 'In the USA, during 2002 to 2007, the top one per cent seized more than sixty-five per cent of the gain in total national income.'
>
> —Joseph E Stiglitz (*The Price of Inequality*)

The project had come to an end. Now Ayan had to stay back for attending the seminar. As the project ended on a Friday, the entire group were taken for a trip to the beautiful, enchanting Lake District of UK. At the end of it, Ayan realised how much the list of his professional friends had expanded. They would be in touch with each other, they promised very sincerely. If this is not globalisation at individual level what is? Surely they may meet each other later during their careers and would happily work together again for mutual benefit.

Johnson had told Ayan that he would have to speak for a few minutes during the seminar. So he was mentally prepared. The seminar was conducted by very eminent heads of big global firms and think tank organisations. The subject "Rise of Asia—Phoenix or Bubble?" was very relevant and critical to global economy in the twenty-first century and beyond. Hence the entire business management world was seized with this opportunity which could change the destiny of humankind for the better when viewed as a phoenix from an optimistic angle. The bubble was from the pessimistic angle. The truth would lie perhaps somewhere between the two. There is a very vast space in between them. That made the seminar quite seamless in its content and context. The presentations and discussions were amazing in their vastness and depth. While the general trend of eminent speakers was positive, lingering doubts about the enigma of China and its ability to lead Asia in such a phenomenal, mind blowing paradigm shift or change were expressed. The expanse of Asia was bewildering, the fault lines were seismic and some of them were explosive. Yet, the general consensus was that Asia's rise was due and inevitable despite all the negatives.

Towards the end of the second day's session a slot was devoted towards asking junior executives to speak for a few minutes.

The keynote speaker said, 'Let us start by hearing a young man from India, a junior executive in GSK. He is Ayan, coming from Prague. Let us hear what he has to say about the subject we have been pontificating about since yesterday.'

Ayan waited for a while, looked around and then walked up to the lectern. He tried his best to hide his trepidation in front of such an array of prominent people. He strode up to the dais exactly as he had mentally rehearsed it. He looked around at the audience in front of him, turned his head towards the collection of elderly and eminent speakers from the business world sitting on the stage with a nervous smile and spoke.

'Ladies and Gentleman, it is indeed a great opportunity for us junior executives to be exposed to such an event where we get to hear from the doyens of the world of business academics. Let me confess the obvious to you all. I am really nervous to speak in front of you. (Laughs)

'The Asian century is plausible. It is not preordained. If India and China don't shed their differences, if India-Pakistan rivalry continuous, if China displays and flexes its vast hard power, if the two Koreas do not mend relations, if Japan and China do not bury their past, then the plausibility will dither and dwindle.'

He paused, looked at the audience, looked towards the panel of speakers again as if to draw some inspiration. They all looked circumspect and attentive. He took off again, no longer nervous now.

'Asia's rise will not be dependent on the thin lifeline of perceived past injustices perperated on China or elsewhere. All nations of Asia have their own persecution complex. Asia has to grow out of this mindset to rise again. India too must stop pretending that its ocean of excluded millions of abject poor are all happy, alive and kicking or that there are as many Gandhis as seen on the currency.

Asia has to draw a clear line between civilization and barbarism and ensure that religion per se not allowed to become a chronicle of bloodletting. Killing each other in the name of religion is a lunatic battle, a display of religious jaundice. We should not allow this to become the Asian Earthritis and I spell 'e a r t h r i t i s'.

'The worst analysis of Asia's rise will be to base it upon the expectation of the ebbing power of the West. No one is going down. No one needs to go down. There are nations in Asia where corruption is deeply entrenched at all levels of society. If that seems so ineradicable, so as to degenerate from being an exception to the rule to become the rule itself, then far from a century, even a decade will not belong to them.

'What Asia or the East needs is not democracy or capitalism. The issue is no longer binary. The rise of Asia is about rising aspirations of the fourth and fifth generation Asians who will have to live their lives through this century. What the East needs is the doctrine of righteous governance while upholding law and order strictly, and a passionate belief in the multiplicity of faiths. We are the principle stakeholders of this paradigm change.

'Yes, we are dreamers and our dreams may sound simplistic. But our dreams are positive. We do not dream of subduing fellow nations, cultures or systems for that will take us all down the abyss of failure. Such horrific dreams are raising their hydra-heads in a few regions of the world including Asia. The rise of evil has to be conquered. We can make Asia rise largely, positively and be able to handle those aspects which are not good in a collective sense. However, we are aware that the twenty-first century will also be an age of frenzy, strife and conflict. We in Asia, particularly, as also in the West, have to invoke the Buddha in us. There need neither be Westoxification of the East nor Eastoxification of the West. Toxins and progress are antithesis of each other.

'Finally, Asia is in the process of creating a new narrative. We the young generation of Asians will create this new narrative. The issue is for you, the elder generation, to lead and guide us with the huge wisdom at your disposal and enable us to do so, with minimal strife and turmoil. So we all here are stakeholders in the creation of a better world which includes the rise of Asia. The starting point of love for humanity is love for your future generations, isn't it? We need that today more than anything else. The emergence of Asia as a huge, stable, economic arena will make the world better. So its rise will not be as dramatic as that of a phoenix nor as bad a disaster as a bubble. It will be as it should be. It will be *que sera, sera*. Thank you all.'

Ayan waited anxiously for a few questions from the eminent people around. A gentleman in a black suit, suave, with a grim visage got hold of a mike and asked, 'Young man, what is it that bothers you about India in this century?'

Ayan paused for a few seconds, scanned the audience and then looked at the gentleman. 'Sir, in a nutshell I would say that when a segment of the nation becomes super rich well before the nation becomes big, then the situation tends to become very combustible. Prime Minister Nehru with great wisdom said in 1947 that the soul of the nation long suppressed would find utterance. The world was impressed. But nearly seven decades later, we are a nation of ebullient talkers and mushrooming think tanks of different grades. Today we have a twenty-first Prime Minister who is trying to concentrate on delivery of good governance. He needs the full support of all, including the fringe elements, both within and outside his own party. If he is not adequately supported, then most of the progress made so far by the nation will belong to the exclusive few and will be inherited by their future generations. That is what bothers my generation of Indians. The price of such gross inequality will be very high.'

A middle aged, eminent lady asked the next question. 'How does your generation perceive the aspect of bad governance as a major headwind to the rise of Asia?'

'Most of us feel strongly that bad governance results in greater casualities than terrorism, both in numerical terms, as well as in its geographical spread. Hundreds of millions die due to effects of extreme poverty every year. So governments which fail miserably to govern and deliver cause grave human distress. Therefore, not a single decade of this century should be wasted in any country of Asia. To end my response, I would only add that a nation like India, and perhaps others too, need to be precise and careful about overvaluing what they are not, as well as undervaluing their strengths .' A bell sounded, signifying that the time had come for the next speaker.

A scholarly lady asked, 'Young man you are from an eminently democratic nation. Do you feel that ushering in democracy all over could make the globalising world better?'

Ayan pondered for a while.

'The essence of democracy is the right to choose. So, by its very core value, it cannot be enforced. Even though democracy is perhaps a great thing, this system has a lot of scope for reformation and cannot be straight–jacketed to fit all sizes. Moreover, you may build a nation on the edifice of democracy, but the foundation of political parties is always based on undemocratic means to gain power. It is a tough call to be worthy of classical democracy. Perhaps, the delivery of good governance is the challenge which transcends the system of governance. In a democracy, if there occurs a situation of choices, then that nation should introspect about deserving democracy itself. I beg your forgiveness if I have messed up my answer.'

A bout of laughter engulfed the hall. Then, a few from the audience clapped and that gained momentum.

A grim looking gentleman in a dark suit asked a very penetrating question. 'How much are you concerned about the complex inter-religion relationship in India?'

There was a hush of silence in the hall. Probably no one expected that a young man would be asked such a question amidst the prevailing academic atmosphere of the event. Ayan smiled, liking this question, however unexpected.

'As a globalised Indian of my generation, I have no doubts that no faith can be controlled by a few people. Irrespective of our personal beliefs and faiths, our existence, our dreams, our capabilities, morality, humanity must be allowed to fly freely. We exist because we can think. And Sir, I am the son of an officer of the Indian army. I am glad you asked me this question. I wish to quote a very eminent officer of our army, Lt Gen Syed Ata Hasnain, now retired. He said, 'When India doubts itself, and the future course of inter-faith relations, it should turn to its army for inspiration: there nothing changes, it only gets better.' I would like to state that the twenty-first century will also test our abilities to discover the joys of life in an imperfect world.'

Ayan continued, 'The twenty-first century has to be choreographed and scripted better than the earlier century. Albert Einstein so relevantly remarked, "If you always do what you have always done, you will always get what you've always got." Our generation, who has to live out this century, is ready to change the world as much as it can. We do not want to carry the cross of the past. And finally, going beyond the specific question, I wish to reiterate that conduct of business during this century will have to be lean, nimble and agile. In a lean transformation, the focus is not just on input versus output, but in using the right processes too. In our rush for wealth creation, we need to pause and get back to basic ethics. A no-holds-barred wealth creation will lead to long term disaster. Wealth creation is a strategy and not just a methodology.

'De-globalisation headwinds are also necessary to ensure constant and never ending course corrections and reforms to ensure inclusivity and fairness. While stressing on this point, I am only quoting Debashish Sarkar and his book on *Lessons in Lean Management*.'

Ayan bowed to the panel of speakers on the stage and walked down the steps amidst loud clapping with wobbling knees. His palms were sweating. He was so relieved to make it to his seat. He was surprised to realise how happy he was to see Li Na clapping for him among the audience.

'We now take a Chinese perspective from a young IT professional. He is Mr Wang Yong from DHL. He is here from Hong Kong.'

Mr Wang got up and walked briskly up to the stage, confident and composed.

'I shall first dwell a bit on the historical backdrop to the subject. In the nineteenth century, European powers came to dominate the planet. Europe was practically the centre of the universe. The end of the European century began in 1914, with the gory destruction and mass killings during the two World Wars. Major cross border wars, civil wars, revolutions and consequent erosion of economic power eclipsed Europe. Thus, began the American century. After the collapse of the mighty Soviet Union, for a decade or so, US progressed beyond being a superpower to become practically the only global power.

'Thereafter, the invasion of Iraq and subsequent array of conflicts resulted in the gradual weakening of American power. This led the global think tanks to coin the phrase and chart the arrival of the Asian century. Hence, we should be very careful about this linear thinking that has been in prevelance since the nineteenth century. We need to think about the future, in this twenty-first century, which perhaps is a benchmark century, with more depth and research.

'Asia is huge, extending from the Red Sea to beyond the East China Seas. It has 60 per cent of global population, multiple and highly diverse civilizations, differing levels of economic development and political systems. It would be pertinent to imagine that this expanse we call Asia today, may shrink due to radical religious standpoints. If this has to be, so be it. Progress has to find its own path when obstructed by twelfth century mindsets.

'The rise of Asia is not about democracy or communism. Be it democracy or communism, governance without a moral compass and the depth of commitment to the people is not what Asia needs. "Winner takes all" politics in a democracy is a dysfunctional form of capitalism of the worst kind. The prospects of inequality in Asia can be frightening. If democracy or communism becomes predominantly a kleptocracy, then Asia cannot rise enough.

'To rise, every nation in Asia must always be in search of its next better destination. Every decade will be wasted if the next better destination is missed. We, the young generation of Chinese whether in China or elsewhere, do not care about what is our system of governance or our politics. What we care about is constant and never ending economic progress.

'Many experts feel that China is ambivalent about an Asian century and thinks primarily about a Chinese century. This may not be so true. China too will enlarge its current vision in coming decades. China's worry about a US dominated strategic order cannot be wished away. Since the global gains from an economically prosperous Asia would be too vast, both may assume collective responsibility to make this happen.

'Therefore, "The rise of Asia in the twenty-first century" will be a more apt term than the term "Asian Century", to start with. The collectiveness and inclusivity of this rise of Asia will consume the bulk of this century. Both China as well as USA have enough wisdom and foresight, to ensure that it never replicates the zero sum game, played by USA and Soviet Union in the past era. Let us all say "Amen" to this expectation.'

A professor from Oxford University asked Wang, 'Young man, you spoke well indeed. Can you list a few "givens" about China during this century?'

Wang smiled, thought for a while and said, 'It is a given that China will continue to be a major global power. Its dependency on global resources is a given and hence it will act responsibly on global issues. Its dependency on the technology of the developed world is another given, as will be its thirst for global markets. At present, its lack of soft power is quite visible. China must work on this aspect seriously. The historical baggage it carries is also a given. This will take a while to overcome. At present, this historical baggage is perhaps a big catalyst which motivates China to think and become big.'

Another professor from Japan asked Wang pointedly, 'What are your views on the ability of China to lead Asia into prosperity and peace?'

'Sir, most of our generation of global citizens have started believing that this century will witness groups of leadership, as against a couple of leaders trying to uphold global order, as in the past. These groups of leaders will be close to each other and interact, discuss issues very frequently. Therefore, perhaps global order, regional order and cohabitating due to the compulsions of mutual interdependence, maybe more in fashion. Such groups of leaders who are constantly in touch with each other on all complicated issues will be displaying more collective and responsible leadership than hitherto. The common existential challenges that they will face in this century will ensure that this paradigm shift happens.'

After the conclusion of the international seminar, both Ayan and Wang were applauded by all the speakers as well as the highly informed people attending it as audience. They all acknowledged the fact that the fourth and fifth generations of Asians as represented by Ayan and Wang were ready for the rise of Asia. They only needed to be given a role as major stakeholders for the 'Asian Sunrise.'

As the attendees of the seminar were chatting with each other over lunch in the adjacent massive central hall, a huge slide was flashed on the screen dominating the hall.

TWENTY-FIRST CENTURY GLOBE—SOME POSSIBILTIES

SOME NEGATIVES

- Half of Amazon rainforests deforested.
- Fish body size declined by a quarter.
- Rainfall intensity increased by 20%.
- Global average temperature up by $3^{0\,C.}$
- Enormous crop shortfalls and war over fresh water.
- Rising religious intolerance, radicalism in some regions.
- Global Nuclear War.
- Asteroid collisions.
- Long term global pandemic.

SOME POSITIVES

- High tech intelligent buildings revolutionise urban landscapes.
- China completes largest water diversion project in human history.
- All religions collectively work for global peace.
- Most continents linked to each other by land routes.
- Genetically engineered designer babies for the rich.
- Vast majority of countries achieve democracy.
- Global population reaches a plateau (9 billion).
- Hand held MRI scanners.
- End of oil age.
- Mars has permanent human presence.
- Global economic power shift away from advanced economies in North America, Western Europe and Japan towards China, India, Mexico, Indonesia, Vietnam, Nigeria, and Malaysia while encouraging many others to be part of this process.
- India and Pakistan jointly and successfully defeat terrorism in South Asia.

As Ayan was interacting with the attendees of the seminar, he got a call from John. Ayan was surprised. John said, 'Well done Ayan. I just got a call from a friend of mine who heard your talk. He was appreciative of all you said. I am glad to have asked you to attend the seminar.'

'Thanks John for this opportunity. I feel very fulfilled.'

'Ayan, I inherited the ethos of grooming my subordinates from my army life. You are the son of a military officer and I had to do it all the more.'

Suddenly, came the greatest surprise of the day, the icing on the cake. Ayan saw Li Na striding up to him with a radiant smile on her face. She looked as fresh as a rose.

'Ayan, you were wonderful, amidst such important people of the business world. I am so happy. You spoke with great depth in a few thought provoking sentences,' she said extending her hands. Ayan held her hands initially softly and then clasped them firmly holding them for a few seconds more than normal.

'Thanks Li Na. What a lovely surprise. I never knew about your being here.'

'Sneha knew but suggested that I surprise you.'

'She gave you a good suggestion. If I had known you were here, I would have been more nervous than I was,' said Ayan laughing, wishing that he had sprayed some cologne on himself in the morning.

'You were certainly not looking nervous Ayan,' insisted Li Na in all sincerity.

'That just proves the point that I may be a good actor,' replied Ayan smiling.

'Wish you all the best Ayan. It was good meeting you. You are going back to Prague tonight. It is such a beautiful city, I am told,' said Li Na. She looked a bit sad.

'Yes it is. Should you decide to visit Prague do let me know. And Li Na, I really appreciate your coming and attending the seminar. I am told that there are groups of students from a few top universities who also came. This is a nice way to expose people to such thought provoking events.'

'That is the norm here Ayan. I was impressed with the term

Asian earthritis and you spelt the word to ensure everyone got it correctly. Your mention of the words Eastoxification and Westoxification was interesting. The appeal to invoke the Buddha in us, as part of rise of Asia, was impressive. It is also an effective way to heal Asian earthritis. Thought provoking indeed! You do think deep, Ayan, and I really like that in you.'

'My God, Li Na, you have given me enough reasons to remember you always,' smiled Ayan,

'Well, you must do that Ayan,' laughed Li Na shyly.

'I feel flattered by your words. Thanks. I have no doubt that we will meet again,' said Ayan confidently. Li Na just smiled and nodded.

'And by the way, what is the meaning of the name Li Na?' Ayan asked.

She said, 'You are expected to find that out.'

After she left, Ayan asked Wang about it.

Wang smiled and replied, 'Elegant.'

'And what is the meaning of Wang?'

'It means brave,' said Wang.

Naveen Meets Ziki

Naveen felt very happy when he got a call from Radhika. 'Hello Naveen, how are you doing? You must be deep into the world of business. I have no doubt that you are doing well.'

'Hi Radhika! Its so nice to hear from you. Are you still in the process of discovering your mission in life? What about your plans for research on Organizational Behaviour?'

'Naveen, after the fantastic tour abroad, I have now joined IIM Ahmadabad for my research.'

'That is great. I do meet your parents here in Singapore whenever I can. They are fine and they always miss you.'

'Yes, I know that Naveen. I shall be there during the next

break. Meanwhile, I want you to meet someone who is coming to Singapore next month. Look after her and also take her along to meet my parents.'

'Sure Radhika. Since she is your good friend, I am sure she is a distinguished young woman. Lesser mortals are not of much interest to you, as I well know.'

'You and Ayan always overestimate me. But I do like to be praised though. She is Ziki Shaked from Israel. She is an astrophysicist in the University of Tel Aviv. She is coming for an international conference to Singapore. She will stay for a couple of days after the conference to see and feel the place that she has heard a lot about from me.'

'My God, she must be a bespectacled serious scientist. I confess that her profession scares me, overawes me. I am in no position to discuss astrophysics. Anyway, I shall do my best to keep her amused.'

'You are wrong in your presumptions about her. She is a wonderful girl of substance. She is not bespectacled and she is very good looking. The rest you find out when you meet her. And Naveen, take good care of her; you are the second Indian she would have met in her life. You better brush up your knowledge about India, particularly aspects like religion, spirituality, family values etc. Bye and take care.'

Naveen had never met anyone from Israel ever. He looked forward to meeting Ziki. He decided to Google some material on Israel as preparation for meeting this young lady.

A week later, he received an email from Ziki. 'Hi, I am Ziki Shaked. Radhika asked me to contact you. She has told me a lot about you. I shall be in Singapore from 15 September to 20 September.I will be at Hotel Shangri La, which is in the central area of Singapore. I will be very happy to meet you. The international conference is scheduled for 15 and 16 September. I will depart on 20th Best. Bye.'

Naveen worked out a programme for Ziki covering the important landmarks of Singapore. He mailed the programme to Ziki and Radhika. Both replied with the icon of two smiling faces. 'We both approve. Thanks Naveen. Wonderful.'

Radhika had suggested that Naveen need not disturb Ziki till the conference was over on the afternoon of 16 September. However, a welcome call to her room in the hotel would be very appropriate. Naveen complied accordingly and after he warmly welcomed Ziki on arrival at the Hotel, they mutually decided to meet at 5 pm on 16 September.

Exactly at 4.45 pm, Naveen reached the lobby of the majestic Hotel Shangri La. He saw a charming young lady sitting engrossed in a magazine. She stood out so much from the usual ladies of Singapore that he could not resist looking at her again and again. Could this be Ziki? Not taking any chance, Naveen walked up to the reception and informed that he was waiting for Miss Ziki. The coy, pretty receptionist smiled and pointed her finger towards the same lady. Thanking her softly, Naveen quietly walked towards the washroom, combed his hair properly, adjusted his favourite shirt and washed his hands. Satisfied, he came out. As he strode towards Ziki, he watched the receptionist smiling at him. Naveen smiled back. She gave him a thumbs up with a naughty smile.

'Hi Ziki, I am Naveen,' he said smiling, extending his freshly washed hand.

'So pleased indeed to meet you Naa-veen,' she pronounced his name with an additional *a*. Her handshake was firm and warm, depicting a confident person. Naveen instantly liked her.

Her eyes were dreamy as well as piercing. This lady was indeed different. He did not feel awed, but she was magnetic. He registered his first impression to be conveyed to Radhika later. After meeting her, Naveen felt a rush of adrenaline, of positivity. This is so amazing, Naveen thought to himself.

They went to East Coast Park by taxi. They strolled along the coastline of the lovely blue water of the sea. The white sandy beach and the blue waters combined in a mesmerising, soothing blend. What a backdrop against which one is taking such a nice young woman for a stroll, pondered Naveen. 'This is one of very few beaches of this size in Singapore,' explained Naveen. After walking for about thirty minutes, he suggested a cycle ride. He hired two bicycles. The vendor said cheerfully, 'Enjoy the ride La. It will be ten dollars each for an hour. But for you two, one more hour is free. Please show me your passports.'

Naveen and Ziki cycled gleefully. She was really enjoying herself. Her smile and laughter were so childlike and radiant. As they glided on, they could see whole stretches of sea with ships. People were seen camping. Entire families had set up camps that seemed to be well equipped. People were seen jogging, skating. People in Singapore are very health conscious. Numerous eating places with barbeque pits appeared as they cycled on.

'We can cycle on for eighteen miles if we wish to Ziki.'

'Sure, we will Naa-veen. Yahoo…' exclaimed an excited Ziki.

'There are awesome sea food options. Sunset here is so beautiful,' suggested Naveen, not wanting this day to end. Soon, they took a drinks break in a small beautiful seaside café. Then they reclined outside, under the swaying coconut palms.

Naveen looked at Ziki and said, 'East Coast Park is one place in Singapore that is synonymous with outdoor revelry. You have seen the lush green reserve forest trails, amidst the concrete jungles of Singapore.'

'It is all so wonderful Naa-veen,' said Ziki softly, relishing it all. She watched people playing volleyball, cable skiing, amidst so many water sports.

'We shall have dinner in East Coast Food Lagoon which offers a variety of local favourites like satay, barbecued chicken wings etc,' said Naveen.

'Okay, but I am hosting the dinner, accompanied by some good quality wine,' chirped Ziki with the excitement of a small girl.

'Never,' said Naveen. 'Radhika will fry me with her anger. Don't even think of it. You are our guest here.'

Ziki appeared not to have heard a word. She was sitting and watching the waves crash over the quayside.

'How safe, secure are the citizens of this small country Naa-veen! All the men, women, children, grandparents have no fear of imminent violence. Nor do they suffer bad dreams about being invaded, conquered and massacred by hordes of people braying for their blood. How great it is just to be able to lead normal lives. Wonder if you can realise how we Israelis feel.'

Naveen did not respond immediately. He felt bad watching the sad, worried expression so visible on Ziki's pretty face.

'You look so very attractive when you are happy and smiling Ziki. Don't let anything spoil it. I am aware of how dangerously Israel survives in a tectonic region of the world. It is a veritable David confronting Goliaths from all sides, except the Mediterranean Sea on your west.'

How much Naveen wanted to put his arm around her shoulders to comfort her. He restrained himself. Instead he got up and offered his hand to help her get up from the sandy surface.

'You must overcome your fears. This is the twenty-first century and Israel is too strong a nation to be tinkered with.'

'Yes Naa-veen. Are we cursed with being forever hunted?'

'Ziki, after graduation, I was a very worried boy. I had no idea where my life was going. I wanted to do well and make my parents proud but did not know how to do it. So, one day I went to a fortune teller on the streets of Delhi. He had two assistants. They were his two parrots. One was older, thoughtful looking. The other was younger but had the serenity of a sage. As soon as I paid up, the sage remained unmoved as if in deep meditation. The older parrot stepped forward and with a swagger walked up like a model towards a pack of cards spread upside down on a piece of cloth. The parrot picked up a number seven and with the same swagger walked back and gave it to its master.

'The fortune teller solemnly told me that I should find my correct path via a meandering route.' Ziki laughed and with twinkling eyes looked at Naveen and exclaimed, 'This is funny. You believed him? Was his prediction correct?'

Naveen said, 'I do not know. But that sentence about the meandering path proved to be true.'

Ziki turned serious and said, 'Naa-veen, we all meander in life, don't we?'

'Yes, I suppose so,' said Naveen.

Ziki stared at the sea thoughtfully. She said softly, 'You know, every ocean is a mystery. Its vast spread looks so seamless and awesome. Its distance must have looked mysterious to our ancient ancestors. They too must have gazed at it and philosophised about life. You wade into the sea along the coastline as all those tourists are doing. Then you wonder how many far off places the water must have touched in its journey to nowhere. Every ocean, every river, every mountain range has a story to tell. Such stories can never have an ending, such stories continue always, opening new chapters.'

Naveen too stared towards the sea and nodded. The sun was setting and amidst such a beautiful panorama of the blue sea, the setting sun, and colourful tourists enjoying themselves, Ziki looked beautiful, though a bit sad. She kept staring out towards the sea and spoke.

'You know Naa-veen, my mom and dad split up when I was eight years old. I mostly lived with mum till the age of sixteen. I could never get fond of my stepfather, particularly after my stepbrother was born. I always wished that my parents had loved each other forever. Why on earth can't parents decide to part before their children are born? Are we some bloody poultry products or cattle? What sort of culture and shallow family ties is this? Is marriage a bloody joke, a biological experiment? I was a very angry young child, craving for parental love.'

Naveen put his hand firmly on her shoulder.

'You know Naa-veen, many times, as a child, I used to go to a small mound near our house in Jerusalem when I was sad. I used to talk to that mound, imploring it to unite my parents. I felt that it was listening to me, helplessly. I used to feel better after sharing my pain and anguish with the mound.'

Naveen said softly, 'Ziki, now you are a young lady of grit and substance. Get over it by ensuring that you do not ever let it happen to your married life. That is the way forward, isn't it?' Ziki nodded quietly.

Naveen and Ziki reached the East Coast Food Lagoon. Naveen got two mugs of beer and they settled down for a relaxed evening. Perhaps it was the effect of the excellent beer, Ziki's demeanour now become cheerful and bubbly. They discussed movies, Bollywood, shared details of respective families, childhood pranks, boarding school experiences, sports, jokes. Over two hours flew by over an excellent meal. Both got to know each other well. Ziki felt very comfortable spending time with Naveen whom she had met for the first time. She closed her eyes and thought of Radhika and thanked her. She found him a thorough gentleman, a well groomed, well brought up guy who knew how to treat women with dignity. She found in him a guy who projected a good image of India.

Next day Naveen took Ziki to Clarke Quay. 'This is a

historical riverside quay, located within Singapore River Planning Area. It is located upstream from the mouth of the pristine Singapore River,' said Naveen.

'Great. We people from Israel love to see rivers and water parks. Let us go,' exclaimed Ziki with childlike enthusiasm.

'You will also enjoy the beautiful architecture and some great music. We shall cruise down the Singapore River. You will see an array of good pubs. There will be carts everywhere offering ice cream sandwiches. Two of the best eating joints are Chilly Crab Chinese Restaurant and Coriander Leaf Bistro, among others.'

'Naa-veen, you have taken great care to show me around Singapore. Thanks indeed. But from now on I shall foot all the bills. I also have to use up the Singapore currency I exchanged for this visit. No further discussion on this. It will increase my happiness.'

Naveen kept quiet, then asked, 'What did you do this morning Ziki?'

Ziki said excitedly, 'Oh, I walked around the streets, business centres, parks etc. I also went to Singapore Management Academy, where my dear friend Radhika and you all did your MBA. Radhika told me a lot about the life there. It is such a lively, throbbing academic institution.'

The evening spent in Clarke Quay was very enjoyable. Naveen found Ziki so unpretentious, warm and genuine. He was already feeling that she would be gone very soon. This was his first interaction with someone from Israel. He had already become very fond of her in a strange way. The cruise on the River Singapore was very enjoyable. The crowd of tourists who boarded the vessel were an exciting lot. There were Singaporeans, Malays, Indians, Europeans, Americans, Japanese and Koreans—a veritable global salad bowl. There was singing, laughter and frolic, with everyone enjoying with gay abandon, relishing and appreciating the views around. Splendid architectural views along the waterway were being photographed with enthusiasm. Ziki was excited to see fun seekers hurling themselves into the sky in a reverse bungee catapult on the seas. For snacks and tea, Naveen took Ziki to the Coriander Leaf Bistro. Ziki was impressed.

'This place markets itself as Singapore's new Asian food hub. The menu spans the entire length and breadth of Asia—a veritable melting pot of Asian flavours. Ziki, I want you to try out a dish from India here.'

'Okay Naa-veen. What is this dish?'

'It is called Masala Dosa. It is like a wrap of sorts. They cook it with olive oil here. Let me see how you like it. I am ordering one. It is big in size. We shall share it, just in case you don't like it. I shall direct them not to put chillies. Then we shall try a snack called idli.'

'That is great. Then we can have some coffee, I suppose.'

'Yes, sure Ziki.'

To Naveen's great relief, Ziki relished the dosa and the idli.

'Dosa was superb and pidly too was great,' she announced.

'It is called idli, not pidly,' replied Naveen laughing.

For dinner, he took her to an excellent place called 'Little Saigon Restaurant'. It offered the best Vietnamese food. The place was beautifully lit with plenty of hanging lanterns and imaginatively designed mood lighting. The ambience thus created was fascinating and soothing. Music was on at a reasonable volume. The band was playing lively 'sing along' classics. Ziki felt mesmerised, watching many diners swaying with the music as they sat listening. Some of them were also singing the songs softly to themselves, without disturbing others. People in Singapore always take great care never to inconvenience others in any manner.

'These people live their lives so happily, with no concern about security, indiscipline or any kind of misbehaviour. All this, in an environment of multi-culturalism, multiple religiousness, multiple languages. Singapore is truly Asia, a model indeed. How incomparable all this is to the Middle East,' lamented Ziki sadly. Naveen noted the sadness and decided to bring Ziki back into the present.

'Ziki, this restaurant is famous for lemongrass marinated fish and grilled duck breast. Before that we can savour some delicately cooked starters. I would recommend a Hanoi martini which is laced with gin, orange curacao, lemongrass syrup and lime.'

'That sounds great,' chirped Ziki with a smile that could launch a thousand ships.

'How quickly can this lady from Israel switch from sadness to happiness as if by a switch,' mused Naveen.

The bandmaster suddenly spoke out.

'Dear guests, my team of musicians today will try their best to make this evening memorable for you all. Today I see a fair number of you from the Indian subcontinent. So a Bollywood duet is in order. Sonali, a very good singer from my group will join me in singing a Bollywood song. The tune is melodious and the words express love between a couple. The theme of the song is:-

'Whenever things go wrong, whenever we face difficulties,
You please remain my support, my love,
There is no one else, there was never anyone else in my life except you,
Please remain with me always when the sky is beautifully lit by the moon (good times)
Every one gives company
But you never leave me during dark times.'

'With this backdrop lyric of the song, we, on behalf of the *Little Saigon Restaurant*, wish all love and forever companionship to our guests. Wherever you go from here, spread love and enrich humanity.'

As the duet started, the melody of love spread since the words of the song were understood by all. A young Indian couple got up and danced gracefully to the song. A Chinese couple took the cue and joined in. So, here were two young couples from India and China, very much in love, dancing on a Bollywood song of yesteryears. Language was no barrier. Towards the last stanza of the song, some Western couples and a Malaysian couple also joined in. The singers, seeing the positive response, continued with the song by repeating it. Ziki looked at Naveen with twinkling eyes. Naveen got up and asked her for a dance. Ziki was happy to accept.

It turned out to be an amazing experience. 'Little Saigon', offering delectable Vietnamese cuisine, had united so many Asian and Europeans, all enjoying, swaying, dancing under the mesmerizing influence of a Bollywood film song from India.

During the drive back to the hotel, Ziki was excitedly talking with Naveen. In between she was also describing her experience to Radhika on her mobile. In the hotel lobby, well past midnight, Naveen wished Ziki good night.

She, in response, gave him a tight hug with moisture in her eyes. She could not speak. She just planted a kiss on Naveen's cheek—a kiss that moved Naveen deeply.

The trip to Sentosa Island was on the third and last day of Ziki's stay in Hotel Shangri La. After this, she would go to Radhika's home to stay with her parents. Radhika's parents had offered to pick up Ziki from the hotel at 10 am on the fourth day.

As Naveen and Ziki drove towards Sentosa Island, he told her about the place.

'Sentosa is a very popular island resort. Twenty million people visit this place every year. It has a two kilometre sheltered beach. Fort Siloso is another fascinating place, particularly for kids. You can really enjoy the chic *cafés* there. Sentosa means peace and tranquillity in Malay language.'

'What is Malay language?' queried Ziki.

'It is the language of Malaysia. In ancient times, Malaysia was known as the island of death. It was an area of killer pirates. You will have an exciting experience of the world of 4D entertainment and Aquatic Adventure Park.'

The three outings in Singapore with Ziki left an indelible influence in the mind of Naveen. What a fascinating person to have met. He hoped to get another hug as a farewell, topped with another small kiss on his cheek, at least. He did get both in ample measure when she thanked him profusely before leaving. Somehow, Naveen sensed that Ziki did not wish to get very emotional. Why should such a pleasant encounter and three lovely, enjoyable days spent together end with visible sadness? Why should sadness be allowed to screw happiness? It is so stupid, isn't it?' thought Naveen.

In any case, he was sure that his association with Ziki had just started. He would meet her again. They would remain in touch.

Where will this relationship which has just started, go? Who knows where rivers go as they start their long journey from their source? Who knows where they go eventually, as they join the sea? wondered Naveen. Wow, mused Naveen, This young lady from Israel has turned me into a philosopher of sorts.

Sneha, Li Na, Zhang

Sneha asked Mary Chic for an appointment to discuss her work done so far. She also forwarded twenty-five pages of her draft.

Hope Mary approves of my general approach to the thesis so far.' She dreaded the thought that Mary would not and ask her to start afresh.

Mary could perceive Sneha's nervousness as she walked into her room.

'So Sneha, first tell me how you feel about the subject matter of your research ?'

'Mary, I am frankly daunted by the awesome scope of the subject. I feel that I have bitten more than I can chew. I feel butterflies in my stomach. I need help.'

Mary lowered her glasses, stared intently at Sneha and said, 'I would have felt quite bad if you had replied differently Sneha. I read your draft notes. You have miles to go yet as you have just started on your long voyage. As yet, you have no clue about your destination. That is exactly what it should be, at this stage.'

'Mary, India itself needs 115 million non-farm jobs over the next decade. The challenges are frightening, menacing. Its percentage of GDP in manufacturing is only 16. India plans to raise it to 25% by 2025. Believe me, with the bad state of delivery of governance so far, this figure seems like a pipedream. The manufacturing sector has to grow to one trillion dollars and create 90 million domestic jobs. India as yet does not have a culture and the ability to manufacture world class products, which the world will buy. I am amazed that politicians in India are not losing their sleep over this issue.'

Mary said gravely, 'Sneha, now that you have bitten this subject, you have to start the process of chewing it, albeit very slowly and steadily, in small portions. You need to become more data based. That will need a huge effort in collation. From such collation, your research will actually start. First, you have to compute what all needs to be done without minimizing the enormity of the problems. Then, you have to research on how it can be done at the global and at the national level. You also have to see how much time, in terms of decades, is required to do so. Each decade of successful achievement will help in gaining more time and that has to go on and on.'

Sneha listened attentively, biting the end of her ball point pen.

Mary added, 'The question on global poverty management is not diagnosis, but the prescription. Ultimately, Cambridge University will examine your prescriptions very carefully indeed.'

'That is so true Mary. India itself needs to give jobs to 400 million illiterates, 200 million semi-literates. So we have to go for low -tech skill training, along with low-tech manufacturing. If a nation tries to be strong on the macro variables, yet remains week on the micro variables, then it is only as strong as its weakest link.

'In developed countries, the percentage of skilled workforce is between 60 to 90% of total work force. India has only 5%

of its massive potential work force formally trained, who are skilled . The construction sector itself will require over 30 million additional skilled people by 2022. Such training on a massive scale has to be outcome based, conducted by professionals, private sectors, the World Bank, United Nations and the friendly foreign countries of the developed world. In addition, there is a need for cross-skilling and up-skilling, to make the work force versatile and thus more productive.

'And Mary, I was reading the book named *The Price of inequality* by Joseph E Stiglitz. It highlights the fact that in the USA, during 2002 to 2007, the top 1% seized more than 65% of the gain in total national income. Something like this is happening in India, too. With nearly 400 million abject poor in India, this is a scary situation indeed. Employment generation on a massive scale, backed with skill training is the only option even in a century where robots are slowly becoming a high-tech work force by itself.'

'True,' said Mary with a smile. 'So Sneha, collect data, data and more data. Go to all the global sites and should you have any IT difficulties in accessing details from anywhere in the world, you meet Dr Sreenivasan who handles all IT issues. Your scholarship caters for a few visits to any country, for which you have to justify the need as you progress in your work. Your work has just started. So press on. Do not feel overwhelmed by the enormity of the research. As you progress step by step, you shall see the light at the end of the tunnel and feel better. Be prepared for facing phases of frustrations, those where butterflies will flutter in your slim tummy.'

'Mary, I often wonder if my starting point of the Industrial Revolution for this subject is right,' asked Sneha.

'You are spot on. Carry on. Only brave people take on the field of research. You could easily have taken on a corporate job,' said Mary smiling encouragingly.

Not so bad a start, sighed Sneha, as she came out of Mary's room. She did not look disappointed. Apparently she was satisfied with my introductory draft paper. If I was in Mary's place, I would not have responded as positively as this, given the long study that needs to be done. She was professionally honest in just about approving my first session. She has challenged me to do much better in the next session. And I will.

Sneha Meets Zhang

Li Na returned from the seminar. With great enthusiasm, she described to Sneha how well Ayan and another young Chinese named Wang had spoken. Sneha felt happy to hear about Ayan's performance.

The next weekend, there was a musical evening in Cambridge. Li Na was excited and urged Sneha to accompany her. It was called "Asian Musical Fusion". The event was a great success. It was a veritable feast of variegated instrumental rendition. In one event, four Indian musicians, all in their thirties played a classical combo with sitar, guitar, *tabla* and *santoor*. The music was mesmerising. The Chinese music was a treat, soft and soothing. Five musicians came on the stage with five instruments. Li Na softly explained the instruments one by one.

'Sneha, the first instrument from the left is Pipa. It is a four string lute. See the pear shaped body. It is a 2,000 years old instrument. It has a wide dynamic range of music and remarkable expressive power.

Sneha nodded, as the musicians were settling down. 'The next one is Liuqin. It is a smaller version of Pipa. Then is the Sanxian. It has three strings. San stands for three and Xian for strings. You see the small sound box with it. It is covered in snake skin. The fourth instrument is called Ruan. It is commonly known as a Chinese guitar. It dates back to Qin Dynasty, around 200 BC. The last one is Guqin. It is the most classical Chinese instrument and dates back to over 3000 years. It is known as the instrument of sages. It enriches the heart and elevates the human spirit. UNESCO has declared this instrument as a heritage.'

The renditions of instrumental music from rural Bangladesh, Indonesia, Vietnam and South Korea were all very good.

At the end came a pianist. He was from Oxford. As he came on stage, Sneha squeezed Li Na's hand and exclaimed, 'He looks so much like Lang Lang, the famous pianist.'

Li Na laughed and said, ' He looks a lot like Lang Lang but he is not. He is Zhang, a second generation British of Chinese origin. He is a very good pianist. He lives near Oxford.'

Zhang played a couple of tunes from Abba. It was a perfect rendition and since the songs were so popular, the crowd enjoyed it immensely. Sneha could not take her eyes off Zhang. He looked so serene and calm. He was deeply immersed in his own music. He did not appear to be conscious of the audience. He was all concentration, swaying slightly with the tunes, with a charming smile on his intense face.

In the finale, the conductor of the show appeared on the stage, amidst a ripple of applause. Sneha was entranced. The grace and athletic skills of the dancers who followed was mesmerizing. They seem to defy gravity as they leapt into the air. It was a great experience indeed

Li Na observed how impressed Sneha was with Zhang. She said very casually, 'I know him well. He is doing a doctorate in Oxford University, which he is finishing soon. His dad is a Chinese and mother a British. His parents are a very interesting couple.'

Sneha appeared delighted to hear that Li Na knew Zhang well. She looked expectantly at her to hear something more. Li Na smiled and pretended otherwise.

After the show, Li Na held Sneha's hand and said, 'Come with me.' She led her towards the corridor connecting the entry to the stage, and waited. In a few minutes, Zhang was seen coming out. He looked handsome and elegant. As he noticed Li Na, he smiled and waved at her. He then strode towards her. Li Na kept holding Sneha's hand deliberately so that Zhang would see it, which he did.

Zhang shook Li Na's hands warmly and wished Sneha. She introduced Sneha to Zhang. As he shook Sneha's hand firmly, he tried to pronounce her name, 'Nice to meet you Sne Ha.'

As Sneha nodded, smiling, Li Na corrected Zhang and said, 'The name is Sneha as one word. The meaning of her name is affectionate.'

'That is interesting. Li Na means elegant. Zhang means great. So in this globalised world, I can say that great is very happy to meet elegant and affectionate.' All three had a good laugh.

'The situation demands that we have coffee together. Doesn't it Sneha?' suggested Zhang.

She nodded her approval and they moved to the coffee shop.

Sneha and Li Na spent over an hour in the coffee shop with Zhang. Sneha was impressed by Zhang's intelligence and excellent behaviour . He was so witty, so observant, so humorous and definitely so very handsome.

A month later, Zhang rang up Sneha. He invited her to come for lunch next Saturday at his home in Oxford. 'My parents would love to meet you and Li Na. We will expect you both at noon. Li Na knows the place.'

Sneha bought a bottle of wine while Li Na bought a perfume as gifts. On the way to Oxford, Li Na briefed Sneha about Zhang's parents.

'You can address his dad as Mr Qiang. His mum is Suzie. They are an amazing couple, so much in love. Mr Quang is a very able dentist. Suzie is a Botanist and teacher in a local collage.'

Just as Li Na and Sneha alighted from the train, they found Zhang waiting. They strolled towards the house chatting, admiring the neat, serene and green environment around with the neat rows of houses around a lush green park. She also noted a cricket ground with a stadium and a bar. They stood for a while and watched. The practice nets were fully occupied by young boys. A big black scoreboard was visible. The fielding team was warming up. A score of men, women and children comprised the audience. They wore colourful dresses and most of them were sipping beer or soft drinks. Weekends in UK are indeed very feisty, colourful and cheerful during summers. Any weekend without fun, frolic, laughter was considered a waste, which is quite unacceptable.

Zhang's house was moderate in size. It was a double storied house with an immaculately maintained garden behind. It had three bedrooms and a study room on the first floor, and was a ten minutes walk from the nearest bus and train stop.

Mr Qiang and Suzie warmly welcomed the two guests at the entrance. Both looked elegant. As they settled down in the drawing room, Suzie brought in a big tray containing an appetizing cake. She gave strict look at Mr Qiang. 'Angie dear, I shall cut a small piece for you and no more.' Then smiling she looked at Sneha and Li Na, 'I call him Angie as Qiang is quite a tongue twister for a whole lifetime. His sugar level is just a shade within the acceptable range. He is so fond of the cakes I bake that he overeats. He even steals a bite from the fridge.'

Everyone laughed. Mr Qiang responded, 'My sugar level is five to ten measures less than the permissible range. She just fusses. So what does the beautiful lady from India think about Britain?'

'Uncle, I feel very happy to have come here for my studies. The environment at Cambridge is awesome,' replied Sneha bashfully. 'More so, as I have a friend like Li Na which means a lot to me. The faculty, the scholarly students are so open minded, analytical and academically sound.'

'Interesting,' replied Mr Qiang smiling. Sneha had already liked him. Mr Qiang attentively watched his wife cutting the cake, laying the slices on five plates. Sneha noticed that off and on he would look at Suzie. 'This couple are still so deeply in love that it shows in all their interactions,' noted Sneha with wonder.

'So, how is your research in English, Li Na,' queried Suzie as she handed over the plates to each one. The last plate contained the smallest piece for her husband. Her husband took the plate graciously accepting the inevitable.

'It is creeping on, slowly but steadily. The literary interest of the British people is so deep and intense. How much they read is amazing! Gifting books to each other is so ingrained in them right from their school library levels, and in their homes. So, doing the research in UK becomes more challenging. How much they remember and respect their literary authors and poets is amazing. The deep appreciation of literature and the correct way of expression is really wonderful.'

'That is well said Li Na. At times we tend to fuss too much about it. To be too correct and rigid becomes a bit boring. In today's age, we could be a bit flexible and hence more adaptable,' said Suzie on a lighter note.

'I agree with you aunty. I would say that today's world is not just a stage. It is an evolving stage, much faster than the Shakespeare era stage. Even then, English is a very fascinating, rich and globalised language. That will not change, ever. Moreover, Asian nations and their people must learn English fast in this century, shouldn't they?'

'True, Li Na,' agreed both Suzie and Mr Qiang almost simultaneously.

Suzie asked Sneha about her research. Sneha explained, 'Aunty, I have just started and presently feel overwhelmed by the enormity of the task ahead of me.'

'That is the best start point for a quality research, Sneha,' said Mr Qiang. 'Be it a subject of Science or Humanities or anything, research is essentially a process of enquiry. It is not a summary of what you already know, with a degree of value addition to it. Take up the challenge and carry on regardless. You will be surprised at what a curious mind can do in any journey of discovery. Deeper the well, sweeter the water. Go deeper and deeper in your quest, the answers will come rushing out. So, tell me something about India, in reference to the context of your research, Sneha.'

'Well sir, India is politically democratic but mentally it is still quite colonial. Somewhere in the core self of Indians lies a dormant seed. It is the seed of achievement of inner potential. In many cases the seed is in sleep mode. If this seed is aroused, it can take India to great heights, much beyond present comprehension.'

'So what is the major hurdle which prevents the seed from awakening Sneha?' asked Qiang attentively.

'The major hurdle is rampant corruption and moral turpitude,' responded Sneha.

'But dear lady, this is a universal problem, isn't it?'

'Generally yes. Such malignancies of corruption, moral turpitude exists in the western world too, but there is a major difference.'

'And what is that?' asked Zhang this time.

Sneha said, 'The western world is sheltered in many ways in the strong arms of extremely developed infrastructure, institutions, built over the centuries since the Industrial Revolution. It is also sheltered in highly developed and developing technology, quality of education and skilled manpower.'

'Interesting indeed,' said Suzie.

'There is another factor which also bothers all nations, but hits India much more,' Sneha added with passion.

Everybody looked on at Sneha to continue.

'You see, logic and creativity fire human brains in positive directions. Therefore education is the key. The power of education and therefore, the power of questioning, particularly by the youth of rural areas frightens politicians at the local levels. The religious leaders too are afraid of this. To such people, it is the miserable, helpless guys who are obedient, pliable and exploitable. So the nasty tentacles of the octopus-like political and religious leaders hold many parts of the world in a destructive embrace.'

'And the more rigid, dogmatic, the religion is, the tighter and more suffocating the embrace, I suppose.' said Li Na.

'Therefore, more the number of *les miserables*, more is the scope to convert them into terrorism,' said Zhang. 'And India is stuck, dealing with such situations in its immediate and distant neighbourhood,' he added.

'Yes. Therefore, if over two billion out of say six billion humans are not stakeholders in progress of humanity, than we have a very serious existential problem,' concluded Sneha.

Li Na said with finality, 'Someone has rightly said that beyond nations is humanity. If this core issue is not understood, then there will be no nation anyway, because there will be no humanity.'

Sneha pondered, with concern writ all over her face. 'You know, Zhang's talk of China becoming a superpower to correct historical indignities suffered in the past worries me. Talks about India overtaking China and challenging its rise, scares me. Such expressions go against the very core spirit of this century. This is not the nineteenth century. Such rhetoric distorts the idea of the rise of Asia.'

Zhang smiled. 'Sneha, do not bother yourself with such rhetoric. Remember, we, my parents and I are also British citizens. Let us, as globalised citizens, challenge such a thought process. Should catching up with China or overtaking it be India's primary preoccupation? I wonder. The enormous challenges that both face is to lift their vast and increasing numbers of abject poor out of their deplorable state. Let China and India compete on this productive enterprise.'

'I know Zhang. This is so true. The real contest China and India face is within themselves. In fact, no nation today can be like a wheel, detached from its axle, moving along somewhere, yet going nowhere specifically.'

Qiang was listening with deep interest. He responded.

'In fact, Sneha, all educated, thinking people of the world are doubtful and apprehensive about future shape of things. Only the stupid ones are cocksure.'

Everyone laughed aloud.

Sneha added, 'True sir. You are perhaps quoting Bertrand Russell.'

'Intelligent lady you are, Sneha,' replied Qiang appreciatively. Suzie was mostly on a listening mode so far. She was observing Sneha closely. She said, 'Well, I must conclude with a serious concern. Just as medieval thoughts and theologies needed renaissance and reformation, so does the political world of the twenty-first century. In this century, a whole lineage of politicians, rulers and bureaucracy need to be done away with. These relics of the past will prevent the globalisation processes. The twenty-first century should be about global spring cleaning on a massive scale. The issue is who will be the main actors to do this?'

'Our generation onwards, all who have to live out this century must take on this job, who else?' exclaimed Sneha.

Suzie smiled affectionately at Sneha, appreciating her reply.

She said pleasantly, 'If you young people are not willing to take the risk, you will have to settle for the ordinary in future. Someone named Jim Rohn said this, "This century gives you wings to fly." So fly.' Then, in her beautiful soft voice Suzie sang a song by Bob Dylan.

> 'Gonna change my way of thinking,
> Make myself a different set of rules,
> Gonna put my best foot forward,
> And stop being influenced by fools.'

Everyone clapped in appreciation.

Sneha looked at Zhang.

'Okay Zhang, for a moment you consider yourself as half Chinese and half Indian. Now tell me in a few sentences how do you view China?'

Zhang kept a steady eye contact with Sneha, smiled and responded.

'Both India and China believe more in their myths and past, rather than in their respective ground realities.'

Sneha said, 'That was only one sentence Zhang.'

He replied, 'When you view myths as truths, you deliberately avoid the raw truth. You deny greatness to your nation.'

Sneha pressed on. 'So Zhang, who do you think is the worse of the two on this fundamental issue. Be frank and fair.'

Zhang replied unhesitatingly. 'It is India at this point in time. Till the 1970s, China was the worse one. The citizens of both nations, in particular the younger generation, must understand that the greatest patriotism is to tell your respective nations when they behave dishonestly. And Sneha, I wish to add a bit more. This applies both to China and India which are critical to the resurgence of Asia.

'It is good to have more money, greater economic muscle. But it is equally good to ponder over so many other serious issues of nation building, which money cannot buy. Both have a shared interest in growing together, for a better world order. Both are just too large a part of the global population. Sneha, I would now sum it up as honestly as I can. Poverty alleviation should be the primary concern for both China and India. The largest chunk of humanity resides in these two countries. China has to also decide if it wants to be part of global problems and threats or wants to be part of the global solutions. This may be the key issue of this century.'

Sneha observed, 'You can rule ignorance, you can manipulate the illiterate, you can do whatever you want, when a people are uneducated. I read this quote somewhere. Moreover,' she said with passion in her voice, 'when in a democracy, voters start expecting very little from the politico–bureaucratic dispensation, democracy moves closer to idio-cracy. Such a situation must be avoided. Massive skill development effort will prevent such a situation in India. This will have to be done in a couple of decades in this century. There is no scope for procrastination.'

Mr Qiang and Suzie nodded approvingly.

Zhang was listening to Sneha with attentively.

'Sneha, I agree. I wonder whether there was any feasibility of a democratic alternative to Gaddafi in Libya or to Saddam in Iraq, or for that matter, in Syria. Both Gaddafi and Saddam were strong rulers where the people had no previous experience of a liberal form of governance. Both descended into chaos, and even worse, misery. So, straight-jacketing the world with democracy can be counterproductive. It can be as destructive as forcing humanity to observe only one religion, even if it has to be done by the sword.'

'So well said,' quipped Sneha.

'But Sneha, I must confess that I picked up this idea from the journal *International Security*. This particular article impressed me. It highlighted two more very important points. The first one suggested that no nation can provide security to another without being entrapped in unwanted conflicts. The second point was that common security can be obtained when two nations have common security interests. It also happens when one believes that the other has enough military capabilities to deter its main adversary without major direct assistance from the other. Therefore, shared threat and balance of military capabilities is necessary.'

Sneha replied gravely, 'So Zhang, in this context, what shared threats or opportunities will foster good relations between China and India?'

Zhang said, 'Radical terrorism would be a shared threat and benefits of globalisation, the peaceful rise of Asia could be critical opportunities, which should help both China and India.' On a graver note he added, 'Sneha, on issues of democracy, there is this use of the term human rights, cultural diversities, religion, etc. Which school of thought do you subscribe to?'

Sneha replied promptly, 'Zhang, the very idea of belonging to a school of thought perplexes me. Every serious thought is a perspective, comprising of partial truths, personal opinions based on sound premises or at least well thought out prejudices, experiences, personal and national interest etc. I feel Zhang that comprehensive truth is an enigma, something like the God delusion to a thinking and questioning mind. It is a never ending search. Therefore, I choose to follow the principle of "To Thine Own Self Be True", to the extent it is possible. Finally, I would like to stress that if you remain transfixed to a school of thought, you will never gravitate to any college of thought or a university of thought. Thoughts should always be seamless, ever expanding as is this universe of ours.'

Sneha smiled and quipped, 'Therefore Zhang, the twenty-first century may not be a perfect one. Perhaps it will be a much more perfect century than hithertofore.'

Radhika and Arvind

Radhika got a well deserved semester break from IIM Ahmedabad. She looked forward to going home for a couple of weeks. She was in regular touch with her group of five. She was aware of the experiences of Ayan, Naveen and Arvind on their job fronts. This helped her to understand more of the global environment. Sneha kept her abreast of how her research was progressing at Cambridge. During her conversations with Arvind, Radhika was pleased to observe that he had become very much more focused, observant and contemplative as well. He was no longer just a Delhi guy but a much travelled global citizen. He was playing an occasional round of golf on Saturdays and a game of Squash on Sundays. Arvind had expressed his desire to meet her in Singapore when she came. He had fixed up three days of leave to be in Singapore then.

For the first time, after the MBA course, both met each other again. As they settled down in a pub with a gin and tonic for Radhika and a beer for Arvind, he was looking abashed and nervous. This is quite unlike Arvind, thought Radhika, as she noticed that otherwise he looked smarter and more confident.

'So Arvind, you have been mailing me about your good experiences on the job front with foreign bosses. I remember that during the MBA programme, you had more or less decided to go back to Delhi and join your dad's real estate business.'

'Come on Radhika, forget the Arvind as he was then. You judge me for what I am evolving into now. I am a different person. You know Radhika, before coming to Singapore Management Academy, I was a spoilt brat. My exposure was confined to North India in general and Delhi in particular. It was more like a fish bowl existence. Since I was a kid, I used to go to our ancestral home in Dalhousie in Himachal Pradesh. On the walls of the corridors there were portraits of my ancestors, all businessmen. Four generations looked down at me from the ornate paintings. They looked proud and arrogant sitting on throne like chairs.

'All such portrayals of wealth, power, amidst vast poverty all around, became visible to me after I completed my MBA here. It was then that I got exposed to the wider world and to you, Sneha, Ayan and Naveen. Your parents are so rich and yet so humble. My dad wanted me to realise all this and break out of my mindset. He wanted me to mould myself as a better person. He was not happy about the materialistic environment in India. At times he would say, "India is too much about Goddess Lakshmi and is getting oblivious to Saraswati, the Goddess of knowledge".'

Radhika was very happy to see how much Arvind had changed. He lingered on the cusp of honest self appraisal. Radhika allowed him to unload himself. 'I know Radhika, you are deeply religious. You know that I am not so. But now I have become spiritual with sound values. I am not an atheist, so perhaps I am an agnostic.'

Radhika responded, 'I too have modified my views on formal religion, a bit. I would rather put this in one's private space, rather than flaunt it. I now believe that perhaps when atheists, who value humanity, outnumber theists, the world maybe a better place.'

'True Radhika. Religious nationalism carries within itself the seeds of destruction, including self destruction. The Mussolinis, Hitlers, Stalins, Osamas will continue to be reborn as modern avatars of their former selves. In this century, the opiate of the masses should be good governance, job creation, health and education facilities, skill training. Economic progress, even if in unequal manner, should touch all.'

'Yes Arvind. That is all true. In the world of today, backward societies are expanding and existing geographically on the fringes of developed nations. These societies are in the cusp of volcanic eruptions, the after-shocks of which will disturb the developed, progressive regions. This is already happening.'

'And what is shocking is that a part of the world population has started welcoming and eulogizing death. They enjoy causing unlimited deaths while blowing themselves up. Dangerous seeds are being sown, whose weeds can only destroy. When religions glorify such mayhem, then we have a harsh reality threatening humanity,' said Arvind.

Radhika said, 'Arvind, ever since the industrial age, to this day, the strong will continue to exploit the weak. So, in this twenty-first century, the weak need to be uplifted. The rich people have to display compassion, charity as well as positive interventions, to improve the lot of the poor, for their own benefit and survival. Those who have more, must give more.'

'That is the point, Radhika. There were people like Kofi Annan who did a lot for the poor. Marianne Cope cared for lepers in an island near Hawaii. Then, we had Pierre Toussaint, a former slave who became a great philanthropist for homeless immigrants. Bono was a famous musician from a group called Rock Bands U2, who used up most of his fortune to help the poorest of poor in Africa. We have Bill Gates, Warren Buffet, Azim Premji and many others who are giving away their enormous wealth to charity.'

'That is so very true, Arvind. Such things happened in the past too. The famous Code of Hammurabi was written 2,000 years before the Bible. It laid down progressive laws like minimum wages, right to be born a free man, debt repayment, poverty alleviation, no incest etc. We, Indians are very low in the pecking order of doing genuine charity. We lack such a missionary zeal. However, there appears to be a rising awareness towards charity in India.'

'At some point in time Radhika, there may arise a universal religion which moulds humans towards love, sharing, caring. This business of "My God is the only God, rest are all blasphemies" is garbage, used with the motive of gaining power over masses of ignorant people.'

'Quite unlikely, though it is highly desirable,' replied Radhika. 'Even if a universal religion ever tries to demand most of my private space, makes me observe taboos, rituals and tries to control my life, then I would resent it. In this very century, there maybe growing numbers of people who will speak against dogmas, extreme views, which despoil humanity. So, individual and collective spirituality, proper parenting at home, correct grooming from primary school onwards, principled political leadership and highly spiritual guides have to be available to bring about such upliftment of human resources. But is this likely?'

'You are right Radhika,' conceded Arvind. 'Just as gravity supports the universe in its suspended state, spirituality supports humans in their goodness and grace.'

'Dear Arvind, surely you have not invited a lady for dinner tonight to discuss such heavy stuff. I have been hearing you as well as observing you. You are so unlike the Arvind I knew.'

'Right you are. Always the sharp observer,' observed Arvind, 'My intentions are honourable, but I concede that my approach this evening has been clumsy. Actually I am trying to impress you, convince you that now I am much more evolved than I was earlier.'

'But Arvind, why do you need to do that?'

Arvind took a deep breath, looked around as if for inspiration, then at Radhika. He knew that he was about to utter the most important words of his life.

'Because dear Radhika, I want to propose marriage to you,' said Arvind.

Radhika was stunned for a moment then annoyed. Sensing he may have rushed, Arvind added with a nervous smile,

'Radhika, do forgive me for trying to play golf on the ninth cloud and messing up my drive completely.'

Radhika was dumfounded. She had never been caught so off-guard by anyone, except her mother, sometimes. She tried to calm herself down by staring at her drink attentively, biting her lower lip. Then she looked up and said, 'Arvind, I hope we are not getting into a situation called Abilene Paradox.'

'What is that? I read about this term somewhere but cannot remember,' replied Arvind softly.

'It is a popular management theory conned by Jerry B Harvey in 1974. In Texas, a group of family members decided to go to Abilene. Every member agreed to go there because they did not want to offend the other. No one knew much about Abilene, including the one who suggested it. Later the trip was a fiasco and all regretted the decision to go there. If everyone had been more honest with each other and had discussed this thoughtfully they may not have gone there.'

'Okay Radhika. Now that both of us are aware of the Abilene Paradox, we can avoid the paradox, take our own time, discuss and think over this matter, can't we?'

'Nevertheless Arvind, I feel like throttling your neck for such a clumsy proposal and taking me so much by surprise. This is not fair.'

'Radhika, as of now, you only consider me to be your friend as I have always been. You, Ayan, Naveen and Sneha did a lot for me to change my deeply entrenched mindset. You have to give me credit for the change. You have seen it all. So now you have to consider my proposal with the attention it deserves. I am not hurrying you. I believe that most significant events in life have a date and time fixed on them. I have thought this through very carefully. I also know that a lady like you would not like to marry just a rich guy—certainly not a guy whose only aim is to carry on his dad's business. I am not going along that road at all and my parents too do not want me to do so.'

'Despite all your explanations, I am still annoyed,' exclaimed Radhika with a smile. 'So to lighten my mood, you tell me three good, short jokes.'

'Okay, here is the first one. A chap was telling his friend that a lady had asked him out. The friend was thrilled and wanted to know where he went with her. The chap explained that he was then in her bedroom.'

Radhika controlled her laugh and expectantly looked up for the second joke. Arvind cleared his throat and said, 'A lady asked the milkman if the milk was fresh. The milkman said "Yes, it is as fresh as it can be. A few hours ago it was grass".'

Radhika looked unimpressed. She waited for his third joke.

Arvind said, 'A man met a lady at a bar. He said "Hi, I am a politician, and I am honest". She said "Hi, I am a prostitute and I am a virgin".'

Radhika was graceful enough to smile at this joke.

'You have to improve a lot Arvind. You are a pig!'

Arvind laughed aloud and said, 'When a lady who loves ham sandwiches calls me a pig, it is actually a compliment and I accept it happily. Radhika, I promise you one thing–if at times after marriage, we ever quarrel, I will allow you to win by *Duckworth–Lewis* method, sportingly.'

'Firstly, this is as yet a hypothetical scenario and secondly, you are presuming that we will quarrel. A very bad start indeed,' replied Radhika with a mock stern expression.

Both of them laughed.

Ayan Breaks Barriers in Love

Ayan was to go to Singapore to meet a few clients to explore some business matters relating to his company. Sneha ensured that she furnished all details of Li Na to Ayan. Li Na was now a teacher in a prominent school of Singapore.

'Li Na is quite excited that you are going to Singapore. Her dad is a doctor. Her mother is a professor in Botany. For generations, they have been living in Singapore. I have not met them but have spoken to them off and on when she was in Cambridge,' Sneha told Ayan.

Ayan assured Sneha that he too was keen to meet Li Na.

'I suggest you have a good look at Li Na as a person. She is a gem. Though you both are from very diverse backgrounds, if you two factor in this diversity and work on it, it will be worth a try. It is just a sincere suggestion. Take your time. I am not insisting on it. The fact is I cannot think of a better couple than you two. You both deserve each other.'

'How are you so sure, Sneha?'

'Ayan, I can only be as sure as one can be. That is all I can say. But you see how you feel about this. It is a very important decision for you both. So tread carefully. Both of you are very sensitive and good hearted. Maybe, you both need each other very much while living in this vast, complex world.'

Ayan was glad to be in Singapore again. He had so many good memories. He visited Singapore Management Academy and met the professors, the Dean, the admin staff. He always nursed the possibility of coming back to this place a decade or so later, to teach here, if possible.

The evening of the second day he met Li Na at a seaside restaurant. It was a swanky, lively place, quite expensive. As a student,he could not afford to come here on his own. Radhika's parents had once invited them here for dinner. This restaurant was also famous for its music and gaiety.

Li Na was expected at 8 pm. Ayan was so excited at the prospect of seeing her that he reached half an hour earlier. He walked up to the reception. The charming young receptionist with a lovely smile looked up and welcomed him. Ayan introduced himself and said excitedly, 'Look, I want your personal attention. That is because my guest who is coming is very special for me. She is Li Na. Kindly make this a great evening for us.'

'Oh sure, just tell me what you want.'

Ayan said, 'Last time I was here about three years back, the music and songs were superb. The food of course was excellent.'

'It has got even better than it was three years ago, I can assure you that,' assured the receptionist.

'Oh great,' laughed Ayan. 'Can I request for a few songs of yesteryears of Cliff Richard to your crooner?'

'Why not. It will be our pleasure. Can you please give me a few minutes? I will be back very soon.'

The receptionist went into an adjacent room. It was probably the manager's office. After five minutes, she breezed back and told Ayan, 'The manager has great pleasure in offering you both a complimentary bottle of red wine. If there are any specific songs of Cliff Richard, please let me know, sir.'

Ayan promptly took out a piece of paper. 'The songs are written on this paper. As we both settle with the wine and starters, I shall give you an indication with a thumbs up. The songs can start then. And please thank the manager for his help. In fact, I really appreciate your help at a very important moment of my life today.'

'Don't worry, Sir Your having selected and written out the three songs before coming here has impressed me so much,' she said laughing.

Just as he had finished setting the stage for this special evening, he saw Li Na walking in. It was only a quarter to eight. Li Na walked in with great poise and dignity. She saw Ayan and come up to him extending her lovely hand.

'Oh Ayan, it's so good to see you! I was so excited that I reached here fifteen minutes early. Let me have a look at you. You were clean shaven when we met in London. Now, I see a little stubble of beard on your chin.'

'Yes Li Na. Every one underestimates my age by a few years in my office. To make them take me more seriously, I thought this little stubble would help.'

Li Na laughed. 'Not a bad idea Ayan. Your stub makes a statement indeed.'

The lady receptionist came up to Li Na and laughingly whispered something in her ear. Li Na excused herself and went with her. The waiter meanwhile escorted Ayan to a very well laid table, with a beautiful bunch of flowers in a crystal vase.

Li Na returned with an amused look. She looked happy and radiant. Soon a tray with a bottle of red wine with ornate wine goblets arrived.

'Ayan, this is a rather expensive wine. There are many good wines at half the cost.'

'Don't worry Li Na, the manager has been very magnanimous indeed in offering this as a compliment. I really don't know why?'

'I guess something about you must have impressed them very much,' she said.

'But that is not possible,' insisted Ayan, 'I did nothing to impress them.'

'Superb wine indeed,' said Li Na, savouring the first sip.

The ambience of the restaurant was stylish, very comfortable and romantic. Most of the guests were young people, all very well dressed. A guitarist was strumming a medley of popular tunes. Soon a smart young guy came on the small stage. There were cheers from the crowd. It seemed that the singer was well known to the local crowd.

'Today's theme for the evening is about expression of love through songs. I shall start with three songs of Cliff Richard. As I sing, do put your hands on the shoulders of your partner and gently sway along with the songs. You can sing along softly with me. Let us make this evening overflow with love and affection for whoever you are with. If alone, think of your love and do the same.' There was a huge cheer of approval.

Li Na looked at Ayan. Ayan shrugged his shoulders, gave a thumbs up sign and smiled innocently. The singer started his first song.

'All day I'm walking in a dream
I think about you constantly
Just like an ever flowing stream
Your memory haunts me constantly
Shadows fall and I try to drive you out of my mind,
You are no longer near to me,
But my heart sees you there with me,
Every sunset you share with me….'

Everyone swayed along with the song. It was like mesmerising waves of flowing love. The singer was so inspired by this response that he went on with the second song without much of a pause. This time Ayan put his hands on Li Na's shoulders.

'Love me tender
Love me long
Take me to your heart
And we'll never part
Love me tender
Love me dear
Tell me you are mine.
I'll be yours through all the years
Till the end of time.'

Now the singer smiled and paused, during which time, drinks were replenished. He was glad to notice that the crowd wanted him to resume. Just as he started, Li Na gently put her arms on Ayan's shoulders in anticipation.

'Why is my heart so light
Why are the stars so bright
Why is the sky so blue,
Since the hour I met you.
I care not what the world may say
Without your love, there is no day
So love, this is my song
Here is a song, a serenade to you.'

The songs went on for a nearly an hour, with pauses in between. Li Na's face was radiant. She loved the evening. The dinner was delectable. Ayan thanked the receptionist and the manager. They came out under the starry sky which was like a seamless umbrella over the calm sea, dotted with boats and ships of various sizes.

Li Na shook Ayan's hands very firmly. 'You are sweet and smart Ayan. I really appreciate your way of telling me so much today without speaking to me. You did it by getting it said through songs sung by someone else.'

'Oh come on Li Na, what did I do?'

'Ayan, the manager is a family friend. That lady receptionist is an acquaintance of mine. They told me everything. They knew I was coming here for a dinner hosted by my friend from India.'

Both of them laughed as they walked along the coast. For a while both just walked along without speaking. Spotting a bench, they sat down. Li Na was quiet while Ayan was apprehensive.

Li Na looked up at the starry sky, then stared towards the sea and softly said, 'Ayan, are you really serious? Have you thought through all this in great depth? Are you in a state to decide on such a serious matter? Have you discussed this with your parents?'

'That is quite a barrage of questions, Li Na. There will be many more questions we have to find answers to, together. I was never so serious in my life before. Never so far have I seen such a clear view of my entire future life.' He now took her hand and held it firmly.

'Please give me a frank answer without thinking much. What is bothering you the most about our suggested relationship?' he asked.

'It is the immense diversity of our origins,' she replied quickly.

'I am convinced that we shall work it out in due course of time,' said Ayan.

'How?' asked Li Na.

'Because Li Na, diversity and unity have to go hand in hand in our generation, while living through this century. See the many diversities existing within India and China. Yet both are nations which are dealing with it. Isn't it? Management of diversity is an existential necessity.'

'But diversities are serious issues. How does one deal with them?'

'By the belief in our mind that on the surface, all diversities are a product of our mind, perceptions and historical baggage. Deep down there exists wisdom, love, humanity, morality and character,' insisted Ayan. 'This is the twenty-first century.'

'You maybe right Ayan. Things like diversities in terms of geography, history, birth, culture, religion, are chosen for us. Other issues, we humans, at least today in twenty-first century can choose for ourselves.

'But Ayan,' insisted Li Na, 'I am worried, confused.'

'But that is how it shall be, at this stage. So am I. As long as we are in the same boat, let us figure out how to negotiate the choppy waters. We both have our respective families as our support system. Don't we?'

'Yes Ayan,' replied Li Na.

'Of course, we shall talk to our respective parents. Then, we shall discuss this collectively with all of them. Our parents will discuss this amongst themselves. The whole process will be gone through. Our sincerity of purpose, the purity of our intentions will become clear. You think about it. I don't even want any commitment from you at this point in time.'

'Yes Ayan, I understand. After all, as far as I am concerned, a marriage should and must be for keeps. One needs to die, to be separated. In marriage, one has to keep building the relationship, brick by brick, forever.'

'True. It is a path that once chosen should never be walked back. So now, let us both relax and enjoy this lovely walk along the coastline together,' said Ayan with a charming smile.

'Li Na, you need to know about my family. Then you will feel more at ease. My dad is a military man. My mum is a diehard military lady. She had no idea of military life till she got married. My parents adore their two children. I have a very protective and caring sister, ten years older to me. She is brilliant. All that my parents care about is our well being and happiness. There is love flowing in our family. You shall be loved a lot when you come in. I know that they shall get ample love from a girl like you.'

Li Na smiled and said, 'Don't stop. Carry on.'

He continued, 'My mother was doing a doctorate in Botany when she met my father. To be able to be with dad wherever he was posted and later to be able to attend to her children, she willingly sacrificed her career. Her world was dad and her children always. Both of them are living out their retired lives happily. She will always endeavour to be like another mother to you.'

Li Na suddenly looked up at the clear, starry sky and whispered something.

'What was that Li Na?'

'A shooting star. Didn't you notice it?'

'I don't need to look up at the sky to see a star. My star is with me, right next to me,' replied Ayan.

'Slowly Ayan. Remember we go about it, brick by brick,' she responded laughing.

'Yes of course, we shall proceed slowly till both of us feel like building our home together. It is the first priority to ensure that our love is true. That is the first step of bricklaying we have to do.'

'How do you manage to express your thoughts so well Ayan?'

'I don't know. Perhaps you bring out the best in me. Albert

Einstein spoke about the two ways to live life… "As if nothing is a miracle and as if everything is a miracle." To me, having met you is a miracle.'

'Ayan,' whispered Li Na, 'I am essentially like an olive ridley sea turtle. Once I choose a nest, it is for keeps. Please remember this always.'

'Well said. In fact, both of us are human turtles. For us the nest is beyond mating. Our nest is where the beloveds reside forever. And Li Na, we must remember that life is unpredictable. Love may arrive when it is least expected. This is what is happening to both of us. Bliss, happiness, as well as sadness, challenges, complexities, all maybe around the corner or down the next alley. Such is the journey of life. So let us travel this together. We need each other to make this journey enjoyable.'

'I am impressed Ayan. You really express yourself so much better than me.'

'I was never so good at this till I met you. So you must always be with me to bring out the best in me,' he said smiling.

Li Na was in a reflective mood.

'Ayan, will your parents be happy?'

Ayan assured her. 'Give me your hand Li Na. Let us hold each other's hand firmly, close our eyes and see how we feel about each other.'

Both did so and felt reassured.

Ayan said confidently, 'My parents have lived their lives in the environment of the Indian military institution. They are very broad minded. Their priority is my happiness and well being. They will fall in love with you at first sight. My mother has never laid down her head at night without praying to God to protect her family. What about your parents?'

She said confidently, 'My parents were born in Singapore. The family has been here for generations. They are agnostics who believe in humanity, morals, ethics and good living. I do not see any problems, particularly after they meet you and your parents. They only need to be assured that I will be happy and well looked after. So let us set the ball rolling in bringing our families together.'

'Okay, let us sail into the sunshine together.'

'Yes sir, into the beautiful land ahoy!' laughed Li Na with twinkling eyes.

Ayan realised how much he was in love with Li Na.

Naveen and Ziki Pitch a Tent Amidst a Global Caravan

Naveen just could not get Ziki out of his mind. He tried to convince himself that a serious lasting relationship between an Indian and a Jew was impractical. How would his parents take such a proposal? Their willing acceptance was inviolable. The religious, cultural divide was so vast. Ziki's parents were long separated. Her mother was living with her long time partner in Jerusalem, where she was a professor of history. Her father had left Israel and was living in Houston, USA. Such things hardly happened in India. The majority of the children in India have their parents living together all their lives. To them, a divorce is a devastating family event. However, in urban areas and among the more prosperous people, a divorce among the younger generation is gaining a bit more acceptance. Notwithstanding changing trends on this issue, India still stands out in the world as a nation where family ties and the institution of marriage are highly valued.

Six months after her last official visit to Singapore, Ziki

was coming to attend another global conclave on astrophysics. Naveen was thrilled to get another opportunity to meet her. Ziki too seemed excited when she told him about her two day visit.

'Could we spend a day in that place of peace and serenity—Sentosa Island ?' she requested.

'Great idea,' replied Naveen.

Naveen and Ziki spent a full day in Sentosa Island. Yet they felt it was a very short day. They appeared to have so much to talk to each other. They sipped a dozen fresh coconuts between them and fresh pineapple juice too. They cycled again along the same route as last time.

During one of the many halts for rest and refreshment, Ziki remarked pensively. 'If only wars could be stopped.'

Naveen said, 'That is being naive. It is like saying that all businesses can be stopped. Wars and conflicts, are, in their core essence, business activities. Wars can now be physical, economic, cultural and psychological as well as combinations of many such issues.'

'Naveen,' mused Ziki, 'wars cause mutually assured destruction in human beings. There could be a nuclear holocaust or any another holocaust triggered by rabid interpretation of religions, it's so called revelations, and their exclusivity.' She had got his name right now.

Naveen replied, 'Ziki, the environment in which you have lived so far has made you very bitter and serious. You have to drag yourself out of it. You can exercise your choices in the big wide world for the rest of your life. This is the twenty-first century, right? Also do not forget that the least discussed genocide in human history is that of American natives. Wonder what happened to the original people in Australia?' Ziki stared at Naveen.

'Yes, you are right Naveen. Many times, we humans encounter situations where we do not know the answers. There are times when our minds descend from the sublime to the ludicrous, as if in a free fall, from embedded religious doctrines to the manslaughter of unimaginable proportions.'

'Therefore Ziki, why not forget about seeking answers to such questions. Start a new life. Give the next generation the liberty from such anguish. Marry a good guy, start a new generation of free people, of global citizens. You can have two such kids as a humble start.'

Ziki laughed aloud.

'Is it a leading suggestion,' she asked.

Naveen laughed and said, 'Ziki, it is time for the next lap of cycling. And Ziki, on serious issues, never rush through life. Stop, pause, think, analyse, and look for worthwhile friends. Finally, stop rereading the last chapter of your life. Just be yourself, be wary but build a better road map for the future. You owe this to yourself. You are a lady of substance and merit. You deserve the best in life.'

Ziki smiled. While cycling, she was a different person. Her face became radiant and she sang a sweet song softly. Naveen was now convinced that he loved her deeply. Something unimaginable, strange, yet delightful was happening in his life. He thought of his parents. He wanted them to know about this. A little later perhaps, he told himself. I must not rush her.

During a lunch break, over a pint of beer, both started chatting as if conscious of the fact that soon the day would be over.

'Naveen, tell me a bit more about India.'

'Ziki, India is an enigma. One can also take an extreme view and say that India is a riddle, wrapped in a mystery, inside an enigma. I read this expression somewhere. It is so very diverse as a nation but so very insular too. So the fault lines are equally diverse and deep. I recently read a book titled *The State We are in* by Bill Hutton. It explained the idea of a stakeholder economy, stakeholder society and nation, stakeholder welfare system, educational system and stakeholder governance. India is far from this idea of a nation. Is it trying to be one? Well, yes. But it is a slow moving elephant, overburdened with population and poverty.

'I can however say that in terms of start-up world, digital world, space research, its military institution, rich crop of human resources, particularly the young generation, its strong family ties, the ability to face hardships with poignant stoicism by its poor segment of population, it is remarkable. Abject poverty and deeply entrenched corruption at all levels are serious challenges. India is waiting for a new genre of politico-bureaucratic leadership. This process appears to have commenced recently.'

'And what about spirituality in India?' asked Ziki.

'Oh yes, India, despite many problems, is deeply spiritual. This is a strange paradox. India's dichotomy is tantalizingly complex. To experience its spirituality you have to travel to various centres of religions. Who knows, you may do so one day,' Naveen smiled. Ziki too kept up the eye contact steadily and smiled back.

'When I take you to some religious places in India Ziki, you will realise the connection between religion and spiritualism. Spiritualism enriches religion. Spiritualism per se is not religion. It is an inner search for deeper meaning of life. It is a personal, private search, a journey.'

'India has a great mythological past, doesn't it?'

'Yes, it does. Once you remove mythology from Indian epics like *Ramayana, Mahabbharata,* you see super classics, conceived and choreographed by our ancient people who were amazingly brilliant. They understood human nature. Indians were an amazingly intelligent, scientific, spiritual, questioning people in the past. Thousands of years of subordination and conquests, have broken the back of its people. The twenty-first century maybe the period when India might regain its rightful place again. Such is our hope. It will not be easy though!

'And Ziki, many believe that if India succeeds in handling its multifaceted religions, diversities and rise up, then the world will be better off. If India fails in this effort, the future of humanity will deteriorate.' '

'Naveen let me tell you frankly that the only two Indians I have met so closely are Radhika and you. Both of you have deeply influenced me. I find this very strange.'

'Nothing just happens by accident. Many times destiny plays its own role in human affairs. Maybe, we knew each other in a previous life? Who knows such things,' said Naveen.

'This is amazing! Radhika said the same thing to me in Israel,' gasped Ziki.

'Ziki, I would like to take you one day to the spiritual places in India like Dharamshala, Rishikesh and origins of Ganges River. You will experience how religious thoughts relate to nature and its mysteries.'

'Tell me a little about the family system in India. Is it in fact cracking up like it already has in the west?'

'Family is still quite a sacred space in India. It is evolving, absorbing the modern trends and reshaping itself. Some people, due to growing prosperity are aping the west and are going overboard, no doubt. In Indian culture, we are intimately connected with our parents. Most of the parents remain together till death. Since parents in India sacrifice a lot for their children's future, in most cases, children too remain committed to them. Modern Indian parents give lots of space to their children to live their lives freely.'

'Nice to hear such things,' said Ziki. She continued, 'In the modern world of selfies, facebook, twitter, we humans are becoming quite self obsessed. It is difficult to differentiate between the real us, from our filtered, projected selves. Are we on the way to transforming ourselves into megalomaniacs? Are we sharing our happiness or displaying it, as our own paparazzi? It sounds as if in our deeper selves, we are participating in a global reality show. I think it is time we all take a pause and introspect on this a bit.'

'Yes Ziki, you are right to observe this. We are on an ego boosting trip. You know Buddha, don't you?'

'Yes Naveen, Radhika told me about Buddha.'

Naveen said, 'A man told Buddha, "I want happiness." Buddha said, "First remove 'I' that is ego. Then remove 'want' that is desire. See now you are only left with happiness".'

'True,' agreed Ziki. 'You know Naveen, we are like islands in the sea. We deem to be separate on the surface but are connected in the deep.'

'Well expressed indeed! You are quite philosophical,' laughed Naveen admiringly.

'Oh no, someone named William Blake said this. I am just quoting him. He was a philosopher indeed,' she clarified.

They strolled along the coast chatting, laughing and resting. Both were so much at ease with each other. As time passed, both were conscious that their time together was ticking on towards her departure from Singapore. Naveen gently held her hand as they walked along. Ziki looked at him and said, 'To both, you and Sneha, I must have, at times, given the impression that I get overtaken by sadness due to the brutality of my environment in Israel. I am not a pessimist. I may have a soft outside but I am a very positive and internally strong person. I know the value of happiness and bliss. In fact, I yearn for it.'

'You are a very fine, accomplished, dignified person, Ziki. You are so much above the mundane. Sneha and I are extremely fascinated by you, believe me.'

'You know Naveen, after meeting you both, I have realised that when life pulls you down under, you can kick against the bottom, push yourself up, break the surface and breathe again freely.'

Suddenly Naveen felt so overwhelmed with emotion that he stopped and did the unthinkable. He put his hands on her shoulders, looked intently at her and said, 'Ziki, let us be together forever till death parts us.'

Ziki put her hands on her mouth, totally taken aback by the unexpected turn of events. She walked few steps backwards in a state of shock and awe. She did not say a word. Against the backdrop of the blue ocean and the setting sun with her hair swaying with the sea breeze, she looked like a Greek princess. For about five minutes, she sat on the sand looking towards the sea. Naveen just kept standing. He was taken by surprise at his sudden utterances.

Ziki got up slowly. Her eyes were moist. She smiled and told Naveen, 'Do you really know me, a foreigner, enough?'

He looked steadily at her and replied, 'I know you Ziki, as a person, enough. I am clear and truthful in my thoughts. But I can assure you, I never planned to propose to you in this manner. It just burst out of me. I am sorry to have perplexed you so much. Oh damn! I didn't even care to ask if you are already committed to someone else!'

'No, I am not. I did not encounter any worthwhile guy till now.'

'Are you sure about that?' asked Naveen.

'No, I am not sure about it, at this moment,' she said with a smile.

'Good,' responded Naveen. 'So I have hope.'

'No need to be pessimistic but I need to digest this sudden development,' replied Ziki.

She changed the topic. 'Tell me a bit about governance in the huge entity called India.'

Glad for the diversion, Naveen said, 'I can do so very quickly with a quotation on bureaucrats by someone named Charleville Motto.

'To think is a sin, to act is a crime,
Just follow the procedures,
Regardless of outcome or time.'

Ziki giggled.

'Ziki, India, soon after Independence, had excellent bureaucrats who were diligent, efficient and displayed character and moral fibre. Many such people, over the years were hounded or transferred a hundred times. Their problems were intricate and vast. They are not responsible for the massive, unmanageable population. Many were subsumed by the falling qualities of political class. I really thank God that I did not attempt to join the civil services.'

Ziki looked up. 'Naveen, were you serious when you talked about us both?'

'Matrimony is a serious matter. In India, it is for keeps. So we need to talk over this matter with complete honesty, examine all angles and explore all implications and complications. We have just started. I care for you deeply. You are an accomplished person. Think through this carefully. I shall respect whatever decision you make. Feel free to keep this issue open. You deserve to get the best.'

Ziki looked at Naveen intently.

'I really feel you need to rethink about us.'

'You know Ziki, Rabindra Nath Tagore said that you cannot cross the sea merely by standing and staring at the water. We can handle some stressful situations of life with a glass of wine laced with love and trust for each other.'

'But Naveen, you should know that I am not perfect for you.'

'Neither of us is perfect Ziki. We can of course be good, as long as we are joined in love and devotion towards each other.'

'And how do we do that?' queried Ziki.

'By marrying each other and committing ourselves to each other till death takes us apart.'

Ziki said in a calm voice. 'I would insist Naveen, that you take six months away from me, think this over and consult your parents. I owe this to you.'

Naveen nodded with a resigned sigh.

'So Ziki, you feel that you need six months to decide about our future?'

She replied unhesitatingly, 'Both of us should do this. Marriage can never be taken lightly, as my parents did. Thank God! you received such good parenting. You are lucky. That is why you take a successful marriage so much for granted. Please understand my cautious approach. I want our marriage to be for keeps. I put my happiness in jeopardy a few years ago when I had an affair. For me, it is seeking a togetherness forever.'

'Ziki, time has come for you to stop torturing yourself about the past.'

'Naveen,' continued Ziki, looking dreamingly into the distance. 'When I met Radhika and you, a lost Israeli girl saw the good face of humanity in two Indians. The family bonding, spiritual bliss, excellent upbringing, value systems, which I was seeking desperately all my life, I found in you both. If I was a man, I would have married Radhika. Now, I know these were not fluke meetings.'

Naveen laughed aloud and said, 'But since you are not a man, it makes sense for you to marry a guy like me.' He made a gesture like film actor Shah Rukh Khan while singing a romantic song and said, 'This is twenty-first century, my dear lady of substance! Change your environment, your location. Change and bring down the Hadrian's Wall in your mind. Let's pitch our caravan in a globalizing world, till death do us apart. And finally,' he concluded, 'Try and overcome the Holocaust of Jews. There have been several such holocausts. Most parts of the world are even now suffering from the threats of holocaust—the holocaust of bad governance and of religious extremists. Abject poverty itself is the parent of mindless violence and crime. Such is the world we are living in. And I think we need each other to live in it.'

'Oh my God! Naveen, you are a very persistent person,' smiled Ziki.

'Oh yes, I am persistent on critical issues of life, Ziki.'

'How did you get this quality?'

'From my parents. Where else? My dad served in the army and mum sacrificed her career to look after me all through. My dad led an honest, honourable military life. He was not rich, though comfortable enough to educate me in the best schools. It was only after his retirement that he took up a job in the civilian world to enable him to build a house to live his post retirement life.'

'I am so happy to hear you say this about your parents. Believe me, Naveen, very few people in developed countries would say what you just said.'

As Ziki concluded, her face was sad.

'Ziki, once your mind is clearer on this issue, I would ensure you meet my parents. As far as I am concerned, it is time I spoke to them.'

'Hope your parents don't get a shock?'

'I do not think so. In the army, parents have hearts and minds that are very broad based. They only want their children to be happily married forever, just as they were. A crisis in the married life of their children is the only adversity they are unable to face. I may have criticised my country on many issues unhesitatingly, but the soft power of India is world class, unmatchable.'

Ziki smiled and looked intently at Naveen.

'Please realise Ziki, Israel maybe a small nation of eight million people but it packs quite a punch. It is a forever ready nation. An organised minority can take on a disorganised majority.'

Ziki nodded in agreement, confidently.

Naveen continued, 'The entire human race can ask so many questions about its misdeeds, so do not think you Israelis are alone in this respect. Why didn't the Germans question Hitler's Holocaust? Where was God during the horrible massacre? Why didn't the Indian philosophers or god-men question the unfair practice of the caste system, about the inhuman system of untouchability? Why did not the Chinese people question the mass massacre caused by Mao during the Cultural Revolution? Why did not the civilized, educated, brilliant British, question the unfairness of the unbridled colonisation of vast parts of the world? Why did not the Americans, from the land of liberty, question the immorality of slavery till Lincoln spoke against it? So dear ZIki, it was never a perfect world.'

It is wonderful when two vastly different cultures try to blend with each other, she thought.

Candid Blend of Two Cultures

Ayan and Li Na got married and settled down in Singapore. Ayan had discussed his love for her with his parents in great detail. His dad had said, 'Ayan, you have to convince your maa and me that you two shall always and forever be happy together. Marriage is too serious an issue. Convince yourself that it is love and not infatuation.'

'Baba, maa,' said Ayan emphatically, 'We have really thought through our life together. Just do not worry about the sincerity of our feelings for each other.'

'In that case, we need to go to Singapore and meet Li Na and her parents,' said his mother.

'That will be very apt, maa. You and baba will be pleased to meet her parents. They are more Singaporean than Chinese. They are quite global and not encumbered by fringe issues. Do not worry. Soon you will meet Li Na, talk to her and interact with her for a few days. I bet you both will compliment me on my choice.'

Maa patted Ayan's cheek affectionately.

'Ayan, we have no doubts that Li Na is a very lucky lady to be marrying you. All we now want to assure ourselves is that our son is also equally lucky to be marrying her. As parents, that too as Indian parents, it is our duty to ensure this. Nothing is more sacred and more crucial than a happy, blessed marriage.'

Meanwhile, Ayan's sister Dia sent him an old letter written by their dad ten years ago to his son-in-law Nilesh. He had slipped it into his jacket pocket while Dia and Nilesh were departing for London after their marriage. The letter read :

> 'We are giving our world to you. Please make sure that it always remains beautiful. We are giving our beloved princess to you. Please make sure that now, she becomes your queen. She will light up your life and will become an ideal wife and mother to your children. She will motivate you to do your best and willingly sacrifice her own career, which she has built up through dedicated studies, whenever required. This is what her mother did earlier.
>
> 'In return, all you have to do is to love and respect her and that dear Nilesh will be the easiest thing for you to do. So I am not asking for much. She is very loving and devoted. So be sensitive and caring. She will love it that you care for her deeply. Remember this particularly when she is unwell or worried. Later in life, if you are lucky to possess a daughter like mine, you shall realise what I mean today. May God bless you with such a daughter. And when you shall give her away in marriage, you too shall request all this of your son-in-law, just as I do so now.'

Arvind and Radhika too got engaged.

Naveen and Ziki decided to get married. In a great display of parental responsibility, Ziki's estranged parents decided to give away their daughter in marriage. Both of them cried a lot when in true Indian style Naveen and Ziki walked around the fire seven times and Naveen chanted the Vedic mantras in which he promised to the almighty that he would look after his wife forever.

The group of five Indians who had entered the Singapore Management Institute to do their MBA course in 2008 had emerged as true global citizens. They were set to face and lead a great life, amidst all the vast possibilities as well as challenges of the twenty-first century. They would happily contribute towards a future in which both India and the larger world order would be better than before. Despite their broadened view of the world, they were deeply patriotic and would always try to enhance the image of India in the eyes, hearts and minds of foreigners. They would do this by dint of their character, morals, efficiency and good values.

'India and China are each other's opportunities, not threats'.
(Chinese Statement After BRICS Summit 2017)

When the ongoing crisis in the Doklam area of the tri-junction between India, China and Bhutan erupted, while at the politico–strategic level, the crisis was finally well managed by the leaders of China and India, a lot of ill will and diatribes were spread via the social media of both sides. The two principal Asian nations came precariously close to a military engagement, in the second decade of the twenty-first century. This would have prevented, to a large extent the process of the rise of Asia as well as globalisation. However, the scars of Doklam will fester for a long time.

The incident affected both Sneha and Zhang adversely. This became evident when they discussed this grave issue over coffee in a restaurant in London. Zhang looked stressed, irritable for the first time. Sneha noticed this. An expression of perplexity came over her face. Zhang was not smiling, he was not his usual self and he was not looking at Sneha directly.

'What is the matter Zhang? Why are you looking so lost?'

'Sneha, this arrogance displayed by India in the Doklam region is highly provocative. It is an issue between China and Bhutan anyway.'

'But Zhang,' responded Sneha, 'wait for some more time. The details and facts on the ground are not clear yet. Do realise that Doklam threatens the entire North East India. It was a grave provocation. Surely it will be resolved in a mature manner. Of late, there are a series of issues, which have surfaced like India's entry into the Security Council on an equal status as China, the NSG membership and terrorism etc. Aren't such differences part of the process of globalisation and its complexities?'

'But Sneha, India is not as yet on par with China. The reality is that whatever India achieves, China does it much quicker and more efficiently, without much cacophony and drama.'

'Come on Zhang. Why are we falling into this type of political discourse and making things personal?'

'But Sneha, India has too much catching up to do before trying to equate itself with China. To reach this level as a global power, China has sacrificed so much, suffered such historical injustices.'

Sneha was stupefied. She had never expected such an outburst from Zhang. She had assumed that Zhang was a classical globalised citizen. For a few minutes both kept quiet. Sneha needed a break to recover from the shock. She took a deep breath, looked at Zhang and spoke calmly and firmly.

'Zhang, I feel you are overwhelmed by the media generated micro view of a situation which demands a macro perspective, that is far larger and deeper understanding and reflection.'

Zhang looked at Sneha as if waiting for more clarification.

She continued on a grave note.

'Maybe Zhang, we need to be cautious about embracing some of the biggest lies of history in the century we live in. Can we, the globalised young generation, at least admit that many of our entrenched beliefs, mindsets were wrong? Do we really know—can we ever know what powerful nations do, what they employ in quest of global domination? Communists, Leftists pretend as if the meek, the working class are going to inherit the earth one day and throw out the evil capitalist. The capitalists aspire to democratise the entire planet wherein the people are liberated from authoritarian Communists and get voting powers. Leftists justify past purges, revolutions, killing of millions as regrettable necessities for the dawn of a new era. Who the hell ever admits that they were wrong? Millions of people died in China in the twentieth century, after the Second World War and at the end of colonialism. No, this time the Japanese did not slaughter the Chinese. Powerful Chinese leaders did this to their own people.' Sneha paused, to calm herself.

She was breathless and pale.

Zhang chipped in excitedly.

'Now Sneha, you are sounding like a Communist basher.'

Sneha responded, 'That is because I have not finished. 'Can India and Pakistan admit to their blunders during partition wherein millions of helpless humanity was slaughtered? Can India admit that due to abject corruption, inadequate delivery of good governance, millions of poor, impoverished, men, women and children die every year? All such sufferings are inflicted under the mask of a throbbing democracy. Can our generation of Pakistanis admit to their error of believing in the radicalized interpretations of their religion? Similarly, can the same generation of Indians question some actions of the fringe elements in this twenty-first century? So Zhang, every generation so far, lived and embraced so many lies including the lies generated from the radical interpretations of religions.

We have to live in this century. Can we admit our errors and eliminate the concept of "your truth versus my truth"?'

Zhang looked at Sneha and tried to smile. Sneha missed the earlier smiling Zhang.

'Okay Sneha, I get your point. However, I feel India is rather jealous of the phenomenal rise of China.'

Sneha was now calmer.

'Zhang, the problem facing the world is not about the phenomenal rise of China. It is a legitimate, well deserved reality. No nation with even elementary wisdom will ever discount this. It is the fear that China instils in the its immediate neighbours, as well as far - off regions. No super power in this century, and mind you there are a group of them, must shape a set of global rules, which only suit them. They have to be based on rational, fair, shared co-prosperity. Such should be the configuration of globalisation, such that the global train has most of humanity on board. We must dream of a global caravan wherein many more tents can be pitched. We, the young generation must dream anew and not get swayed by powerful political leaders and business honchos who will perhaps only survive a decade more.'

Now Sneha felt drained out. She needed to rush to the washroom. She excused herself. The restaurant was throbbing with activity. Scores of tourists and weekenders were enjoying themselves, keeping the waiters very busy.

As she came out of the washroom, she suddenly decided to rush out quickly before Zhang spotted her. She came out of the restaurant and hailed a taxi. She had to get away fast. She messaged Zhang explaining her reasons for such behaviour. She started crying softly. Then suddenly, and very decisively, she typed another message saying, 'Zhang, we need a break. Can we be on our own for two weeks and reflect? We both need to.'

Exactly after two weeks, Sneha got a call from Zhang.

'Hello Sneha. The quarantine of two weeks is over. I owe it to you to invite you for coffee and sandwiches.'

Sneha replied, 'Sure Zhang. I too want to meet you.'

'So let us meet at a better place than last time.'

'No Zhang. Please let us meet at the same place.'

Zhang agreed. The two friends met in a more relaxed manner.

Zhang smiled and quipped, 'So dear Sneha, the Doklam issue has been amicably resolved. Both sides handled the situation in a mature manner.'

She replied thoughtfully, 'Yes, but this development hides more than it reveals Zhang. Why should it have occurred in the first place? I am sceptical. I am very worried too. It was like a hurricane, which came menacingly close and suddenly petered out.'

Zhang was more reconciliatory.

'Come on Sneha. Do not delve so deeply into this subject.'

'But Zhang,' pleaded Sneha, 'We two did get swept by the hurricane, much before it petered out. Didn't we? I am very concerned.'

'Concerned about what Sneha?'

'My brother is a young Major in the Indian army. He is there right on the border, at the tri-junction. He is very young. I too wanted to join the army very much, but my parents did not allow me.'

Zhang was stumped. He had not foreseen this reality. He looked at Sneha helplessly. Suddenly he realised that both of them belonged to two very diverse cultures and ecosystems.

As if reading his mind, Sneha said gently, 'Dear Zhang, I have been doing deep introspection since we last met. India is a diverse, democratic and cacophonic nation. Such a system will be less efficient than a totalitarian nation like China. We

Indians never think the same way or hold same opinions. We accept, and at times tolerate diversity as a way of life. China is different. To us it seems that in China people have no right to think differently on national, religious or cultural issues and certainly not on political issues. In India, we cannot believe in a society with uniformity in thinking. We feel that such a society will be brain dead.'

Zhang stared at Sneha with deep respect. For a few minutes, both sipped their coffee, staring towards the Thames River quietly.

Zhang said with a sigh, 'It is unfortunate that China and India are getting so adversarial of late. Are we victims of the past century? So what,if we were at war in 1962? So what, if there are some areas where our interests clash? Which two countries with such vast and complex border and history do not have issues to resolve? After all, the alignment of borders was done when both countries were under colonial domination.'

Sneha said, 'Dear Zhang, I am more disturbed with the reality that during our last discussion on this subject, a couple of weeks back, you and I got heated up. We did not discuss this as responsible global citizens. Suddenly we became Chinese and Indian and therefore were quite blinkered.'

For a few minutes both kept quiet. Sneha broke the silence.

'Is the past of such great importance? Isn't the present more important? But in the final analysis, it is the future we have to deal with. Must we perpetuate the present?'

She continued with greater passion. 'Zhang, the past is something we should not worry about. The present too is, in many aspects not what it ought to be. It is the future that authors, analysts, thinkers, global leaders etc. are more concerned with. So why should our generation carry forward the baggage of the past?'

Zhang spoke earnestly, 'Sneha, perhaps the process of

designing the future necessitates thinking critical aspects of nationhood and each nation has the right to decide how to mould its own people.'

Sneha looked bewildered.

'Zhang, you really mean that rulers of a nation know best how to "mould" its own people, their minds, hearts and their existence, per se. You support the North Korean system?'

'Oh no ! I am talking about China. The young generation of mainland China have no problems with their form of governance.'

'I am not sure of this Zhang. Yes, a particular segment of young, rich Chinese, are beneficiaries of 'One Child Policy.' They have inherited lots of property. Do they represent the majority? But, that is not the point Zhang. The point is about believing in the concept of the permanence of human nature. Systems based on such a concept certainly are more clinically efficient till they last. I believe, that in all civilized societies, democracy is the way forward. Democracy and hence diversity, as you said about India the last time we met.'

'I am sorry to have hurt your feelings Sneha,' replied Zhang sincerely.

'You were right to an extent Zhang. But efforts to ensure permanence and uniformity of nature will always result in revolution through violence. Human nature is meant to be evolving, changing. You were born in UK. Your dad is Chinese and your mother is British. Yet, the Doklam event provoked you to respond to me in a manner anyone from mainland China would have done. I too responded accordingly. We both lost our plot, despite our globalized upbringings. The fact that my own brother is presently deployed in the tri-junction area, made me feel very upset.'

Zhang remained silent. They walked along the Thames. Sneha wondered why both were walking slowly, rather deliberately slowly. As they stopped for a while, Zhang looked at Sneha and said, 'So Sneha, where does our friendship go from here?'

Sneha said in a quivering voice, 'Zhang, we two are perhaps the only casualties of the Doklam confrontation, ironically. I believe firmly that Doklam was the first move in a strategic chess game of this century, between China and India. This chess game has to end sometime later, in a strategic stalemate. That will waste perhaps a decade or more of this century. There will be some among our generation who will not be so affected by Doklam and will move on. We will still be friends always.'

Zhang nodded in silence but with sadness.

'Tell me Sneha, later whenever you get married, would you prefer a son or daughter?'

Sneha smiled and said, 'A daughter. And what about you?'

Zhang said, 'Son.'

Sneha shook his hand and said, 'What the hell Zhang. Maybe, three decades onwards, in this twenty-first century, our kids may marry each other and break the Doklam Wall forever.'

Surprisingly, both were smiling, yet had tears in their eyes, as the sun was setting over the London horizon.

❖❖❖